KU-186-729

BLACK HARVEST

Ann Pilling was brought up in Warrington, Cheshire, and many of her books are set in the industrial North West. She read English at London University, where she wrote a thesis on C. S. Lewis for the M Phil degree. For some years she taught English in Buckinghamshire, then spent time in America before returning to Oxford, where she now lives. She is married with two sons.

Ann has been writing books for children since 1983. Among her many titles are several novels of contemporary life, including *Vote for Baz*, *Mother's Daily Scream* and *Henry's Leg*, which won the 1986 Guardian Award and was subsequently televised. She has also written several books for younger children, a children's Bible and two adult novels. *Black Harvest* was her first published book.

Apart from literature, Ann enjoys music, both listening and singing. If she had not become a writer she would have liked to have been a vet – she loves animals, and Arthur, the family cat, has a starring role in one of her most recent books, *The Empty Frame*.

by the same author

The Pit
The Witch of Lagg
The Beggar's Curse
The Empty Frame

Collins Modern Classics

Black Harvest

by

Ann Pilling

illustrated by
David Wyatt

Collins

An imprint of HarperCollinsPublishers

For E. I. C.
1916–1963

First published in Great Britain by Armada 1983
First published as a Collins Modern Classic 1999

5 7 9 10 8 6 4

Collins Modern Classics is an imprint of
HarperCollins*Publishers* Ltd, 77–85 Fulham Palace Road,
Hammersmith, London W6 8JB.

The HarperCollins website address is
www.**fire**and**water**.com

Copyright © Ann Cheetham 1983
Postscript copyright © Ann Pilling 1999
Illustrations copyright ©

ISBN 0 00 675426–0

Printed and bound in Great Britain by
Omnia Books Limited, Glasgow

Conditions of Sale
This book is sold subject to the condition
that it shall not, by way of trade or otherwise,
be lent, re-sold, hired out or otherwise circulated
without the publisher's prior written consent in any
form of binding or cover other than that in which
it is published and without a similar condition
including this condition being imposed
on the subsequent purchaser.

CONTENTS

Chapter One

"CAN YOU STOP the car? I'm going to be sick," moaned Oliver.

"Not *again*," Prill muttered, under her breath. It was the third time since Dublin.

Mr Blakeman pulled off the road, slammed the brakes on, and jumped out, grabbing Oliver and steering him towards a clump of grass. The sudden jolt had woken the baby and she was wriggling in her mother's arms, making the dry-throated complaining noise that was usually followed by a great bawl. By now she must be both hungry and wet. Before too long they'd have to stop yet again and get the nappies out. They were never going to reach Dr Moynihan's bungalow at this rate.

From the front seat Colin sneaked a quick look at his cousin. This car business was getting ridiculous. Nobody could help being sick, but by now Oliver couldn't have anything left to be sick with. It was all in his mind.

"Please would you move up?" the small boy said to Prill. There was plenty of room but she still slid over towards her mother, leaving a strip of seat between them. Oliver's large pale eyes inspected it carefully, then he bent down and lifted a pile of books back on to his bony knees, hugging them to his chest as if to ward off blows.

Colin and Prill had looked at the books last night, in the Dublin hotel. Most of them were about bugs and beetles, and there was one about Ireland too. Mr Blakeman was impressed.

"Your cousin's obviously been doing his homework," he said. "Look at all these… insects… mosses… *The Land and People of Ireland*… This is what you two should have been doing. When you're going to spend a month in a place like Ballimagliesh, it's as well to know something about it."

Prill was cross. Dad didn't often sound like a schoolteacher, even though he was one. Anyway, she'd been too busy practising for her Gold Award down at the swimming pool to do much reading, and Colin had only just come back from the school camp.

Oliver's books smelt peculiar. They weren't new, with shiny coloured jackets, but musty and faded, and they all had Uncle Stanley's name in the front. That smell had taken Colin right back into his early childhood, to a place in London, a tall, thin house, in a terrace near the River Thames. He could remember a gloomy front door with the paint peeling, and

Chapter One

dark corridors inside, where old men and women came and went silently, like ghosts. He could remember the smell of cabbage and brisk Aunt Phyllis, who looked after elderly people, pouring tea with one arm and jiggling a squalling child with the other – Oliver, the ugliest baby he'd ever seen.

Three-year-old Prill had spent her time scowling at her aunt because she insisted on calling her *Priscilla*, Uncle Stanley had ticked Colin off for sliding on the hall lino, and from their flat at the top of the house that ugly baby had never stopped yelling. Now it was nearly ten years old and coming with them on holiday to Ballimagliesh.

It was the first time Oliver had been away from home without his parents. He'd had glandular fever and missed two months of school. He was extremely thin. He moved slowly and his eyes watered. "Don't forget to wear a vest," his mother had reminded him, shutting the car door. The Blakemans didn't have a vest between them, and who wore one in August anyway? Oliver had carefully arranged his beetle books on his knees and stared at them with cold suspicion. In their bones Colin and Prill knew that it wasn't going to work, bringing him on holiday.

Their mother changed Alison in sight and sound of the sea. She spread an old bath towel out on the grass, and the baby kicked its chubby legs and gurgled while the Atlantic shimmered at them in a blue haze, only fields away.

"What a spot to choose!" Dad said. "Could we borrow your binoculars, Oliver? I think we can see the bungalow from here."

Colin was the first to locate it. He focused on a group of farm buildings then followed a track past a huddle of stunted trees out of which smoke was curling. Between this and the sea's edge was a long, low building, glaring white.

"It's terribly new," Prill said, disappointed. On the way down from Dublin they had driven past so many old cottages, some of them thatched, with wild gardens and hens scratching about, and cats lying on the roof. She didn't fancy a month in a brand-new house.

"It was finished quite recently, I think. Dr Moynihan's only stayed in it once himself, and they're still digging into the hill to make a garage."

Colin still had the binoculars. "Yes, I can see a concrete mixer and a pile of sand."

"I wish you were staying too, Dad," Prill said, feeling unsettled suddenly. "I wish you weren't going straight back."

"If the painting goes well I'll come and join you, but I must make the most of the time with Dr Moynihan. I dare say he'll be going back to America in a few weeks anyway, he never stays in one place for very long."

David Blakeman was an art teacher who really wanted to paint. Colin couldn't actually remember a time when he'd not painted, in the ramshackle sun-room built on to the back of the house. Those were the times he was happy, shut away for hours at weekends and emerging for the odd cup of tea, humming to himself. He liked painting people best. He'd done several drawings of friends' children, but nobody had paid him very much for them.

"You're too soft," his wife was always telling him. "Your work's really good." But he usually shrugged and said nothing. Then, last summer term, he'd had a blazing row with the headmaster at school. It was all to do with timetables. He stormed home and said he was throwing his job up. He hadn't, of course. The Blakemans were short of money and Mum was having a baby. But when the holidays started he cleared out the sun-room, prepared a large canvas, and started an oil painting of Colin and Prill.

Everyone who saw it said it was the best thing he'd ever done. The chairman of the local art group persuaded him to send it to London, and it was hung in an important exhibition. They were all pleased and for a while Dad was more cheerful than he had been for ages. But eventually the excitement fizzled out. He started to think about the new term at Horwood Comprehensive, and gloom settled down on him again.

Then, just before Christmas, a man came to see him on behalf of a Dr Peter Moynihan, an American industrialist with offices in New York and Amsterdam, and a home in Dublin. He'd seen the portrait of Colin and Prill in London and made enquiries about the artist. A month later, at a meeting of his directors, it was agreed that David Blakeman should be commissioned to paint Dr Moynihan and the portrait was to hang in the company's main office, in New York.

Dad said it was a minor miracle. He resisted the

temptation to give his job up but he privately hoped that in a couple of years he might be able to paint full-time. The summer was to be spent in Dublin, working on the portrait, and meanwhile Dr Moynihan had offered the rest of the family the use of his second home.

"It's barely finished," he explained on the phone. "But I'd like it lived in. It's near the sea and I think they'd find it comfortable. If you would like to think about it…"

Would they! Money was tight and the Blakemans hadn't had a holiday for three years. The sun beat down as Dad steered slowly down a bumpy track that left the main road and plunged through a patchwork of tiny fields towards the sea.

It was a superb position for a house and they all poked their heads out of the windows for a better view. Everyone was excited, except Oliver. Jessie, the Blakemans' dog, was barking wildly in the back, and Alison had started whimpering again. Oliver didn't like dogs or babies. Both were noisy and had strange smells. In fact, he was definitely unsure about the whole thing. And that made three of them.

The bungalow was the lightest place Prill had ever been in. Large windows on all sides looked out over the cliffs and the sea, and on the small fields behind. All the paint was white, the colours cool, the bedspreads and curtains sandy browns and fawns.

Colin and Prill went from room to room, peering in at the shining interiors. Nearly everything looked and smelt brand new, though the chairs and sofas were rather angular and uncomfortable. The pale walls were hung with very modern paintings; there was a locked glass cabinet in the main sitting-room, full of porcelain figures, and a collection of old snuff-boxes on a glass-topped table in the hall.

It was the most luxurious house they had ever set foot in, like a film-set or something featured in a magazine. No wonder Dr Moynihan had fussed about everything being locked up when they went out. Mum plonked the grizzling baby down on a thick, cream-coloured carpet, then thought better of it and carried her off to the kitchen.

"How fabulous!" Dad said, looking at the enormous fridge, and the dishwasher, and the automatic washing machine. "You can sit at this table, eating your cornflakes, looking at the sea, with all these machines whizzing round…"

"I suppose this is what people mean by a dream kitchen?" Prill said flatly, thinking about their own small, dark one at home.

"Don't you like it?"

"Ye-es," she said slowly. "But I thought it was going to be an *old* house." She rubbed at her neck. She was feeling itchy, and sticky all over. "It's awfully hot, Dad. Have they left the central heating on, by mistake?"

He was leaning against a radiator. "No. This is quite cold. It's a hot day. Why don't you go and have a look round outside?"

As Prill trailed off through the back door, Dad noticed

how red the baby was. "Is she all right, Jeannie?" he said. "Do you think she's running a temperature? Hope she's not going to play up while I'm away."

"Oh, it's the car journey. She'll settle down."

Mrs Blakeman felt the baby's forehead. "Mm. She *is* hot, you're right. Still, it's a warm day. I thought it was always supposed to rain in Ireland? Look at that sky! I think we're in for a heatwave."

Chapter Two

OLIVER WAS TO share a bedroom with Colin. Without consulting anybody he got his case out of the car, lugged it inside, and started to unpack. Jessie kept leaping up at him and barking. He flapped his hands at her nervously.

"She's a stupid dog," Colin explained, realizing he was quite frightened. Jessie was nearly as big as Oliver. "She just wants to play. When people don't want her she never seems to get the message. It just makes her worse."

"Do you think she's educationally subnormal?" Oliver said solemnly, pronouncing the long words very slowly.

"Dunno. Don't think she'd get any O levels. Well, that's what my dad says."

Then the dog crashed into a table and sent a lamp flying. "*Jessie!*" Colin shouted. The snuff-boxes would have to be put away or the whole lot would be dashed to smithereens. He took her outside and tied her to the concrete mixer. "Stay there, daft dog, till I've unpacked. Then I'll take you for a walk."

Oliver's side of the bedroom was soon beautifully neat and tidy. His books were arranged on a shelf, his bed was made, a pair of winceyette pyjamas lay neatly folded on his pillow.

"Shouldn't think you'd need those, Oliver, it's so hot."

Colin was sweating. He'd already stripped down to his shorts and kicked his sneakers off, and even the carpet felt warm. Oliver looked distastefully at his bare feet. "*I'm* not hot."

He went on reading his book. He was wearing both socks and shoes, thick trousers and a shirt with a light sweater over it. Underneath that lot he no doubt wore thermal underwear. Colin was irritated. Oliver looked so cool, while he had a raging thirst and was sweating like a pig.

Then somebody tapped on the window. Oliver spun round and Colin nearly dropped his precious camera. A big red face was looking in at them and smiling.

Colin tried to open one of the panes but it was stuck. The person outside, a very fat man, with a clerical collar and a dusty black suit, pointed a plump finger and mouthed, "Front *door*. I couldn't make anyone *hear*."

"Oh, OK. Hang on," Colin mouthed back, and went out into the hall. Oliver slipped a marker carefully into his book, placed it on top of the pyjamas, and followed silently.

★　★　★

"You just have the two boys, then?" the priest was saying, perched precariously on a kitchen stool. Mrs Blakeman was opening cupboard doors, looking for cups and saucers so she could make a cup of tea.

"Oh no, this one's ours," Dad explained. "Oliver's a cousin."

"*Second* cousin," the small clear voice said emphatically. "By adoption." He was staring at the fat clergyman, thinking he looked like Friar Tuck.

"Yes, yes of course," the man said hurriedly. There was so little resemblance. The older boy had coarse ginger curls, green eyes and skin like a speckled brown egg. He was tall and well built and looked like a footballer. The cousin was small and scrawny with lank black hair and rather bulging blue eyes that stared at him out of a thin white face.

Father Hagan returned the stare, then smiled, before dropping his eyes. Something in the boy's face made him feel uncomfortable. He couldn't for the life of him say what it was.

"There are two more," Dad was saying. "Our daughter Priscilla and a baby. She's just six months old. They've gone down to the sea for a bit of air, Prill wasn't feeling too good. It's the long car journey, I expect."

"You won't have met old Donal yet, will you?"

"*Donal?* Er, no. We've only been here a couple of hours."

"Well, you'll see him around. But it's as well to be warned. Sure he's a good soul, Donal Morrissey, salt of the earth. But he's got to that stage when the smallest change upsets him."

"Does he live nearby then?"

"So he does. He's your nearest neighbour. See those trees, where the smoke is? There's a caravan in the middle of them, that's where he lives. He's got an old stove; he burns peat on it."

"Is he *very* old?" Oliver said, still staring.

"Nearer ninety than eighty. He was upset when they started building this bungalow. He didn't like the noise they made, or the lorries going up and down the track."

"I'm surprised Dr Moynihan was allowed to build here," Dad said. "I'm amazed the farmer sold him the land."

"Well, the O'Malleys needed the money to get their farm back on its feet. They've had a run of very bad harvests. The house looks a bit raw and new at the moment, but when everything's tidied up and the trees have grown it'll fit in. He's even having his garage built into this slope, so you can't see it. That costs money." He finished his tea and stood up. "Well, goodbye now. I just wanted to wish you all a good holiday. Ballimagliesh is my parish, I'm always around. Mrs O'Malley keeps her eye on the bungalow of course. She has a key. But I'm only up the road, so just knock on my door if you need anything. It's the last house on the road when you leave the village."

They watched him clamp a shapeless black hat on his head, mount an ancient bicycle and pedal away slowly, his coat flapping round him, and his thick grey hair blowing about as he bumped over the stones. He had a calm, generous face. Dad rather wished he could spend the next month painting him, and not rich Dr Moynihan who had a little bald head and wore navy-blue city suits.

Chapter Two

★ ★ ★

Prill walked along the beach with Alison in her arms. The tide was out and the sea a flat blue line edging a strip of tawny sand. She'd hoped for a wind down here, but the air was strangely still. Everything had gone very quiet suddenly. Nothing broke the silence, nothing that moved. There wasn't even a gull to tear at the quietness with its sour, high crying, not even a crab.

She looked back at the steep path she'd climbed down from the fields. The tall cliffs reared up all round, ringing the cover, blotting out the gleaming white bungalow, the grass, the wind-blown trees. She and Alison could have been the only people alive on earth.

The baby wriggled in her arms and started to whine. Prill jiggled her up and down and tried to make soothing noises. "Come on, Alleybobs, it's all right. *Look*. Look at the sand. Look at the *sea*. Bye Baby Bunting…" But it wasn't her mother's voice, and the baby squirmed and flung herself about violently in Prill's arms, then went rigid, like a lump of wood. Her face was bright red. Through the tiny cotton dress she was sweating and sticking to Prill's T-shirt.

Prill still felt very hot herself, and rather sick too. But Alison should be all right now, she'd been fed and changed again before coming down to the beach and she smelt of talcum powder. Prill held her close and tried to comfort her, breathing in the baby smell through the little frock.

Then something made her stomach lurch violently. There was a smell drifting over from somewhere, a rich, sweetish, rotten smell. At first she thought it came from the farm, some kind of fertiliser they'd been spreading on the fields. But it wasn't manure. She wouldn't have minded that. This was too sweet, too cloying, and anyway, it was so close.

With the baby crying loudly and twisting about in her arms she walked slowly along the beach, her insides heaving, looking for something dead. A sheep could have fallen down on to the rocks and rotted there, or it might be a dog, lying in the blistering sun with its back broken, empty eye-sockets staring up at the sky, alive with maggots.

She shuddered, feeling for a handkerchief to put over her nose, but she couldn't find one. So she thrust her face close to the baby and breathed in her smell, trying to blot out whatever it was that made her stomach lurch about and brought vomit into her mouth.

For a minute she thought the smell might be coming off the sea. It could be seaweed, piled up by the water along the tideline, steaming in the sun. But the pale sand was quite bare, and when she turned and looked back at the cliffs it met her again, sweeping over her in great waves, making her insides heave.

What on earth was it? Bad meat? Just a farmyard smell? Or was it rotting vegetation, something like leaf mould? But no garden had ever smelt like this and anyway, how could it be any of these things on a lonely beach, miles from anywhere?

Alison was now screaming hysterically. Hanging on to her with one arm, and with the other across her face to stop the smell, Prill stumbled, choking, back along the beach, towards the cliff path. The baby must have some bug that was making her peevish, she was usually so good-tempered. And Prill must have caught it too. That would be why she felt so sick and hot and kept imagining this awful smell.

She clambered up the track towards the bungalow, trying to tell herself firmly that everything was all right. But fear gnawed at her. She had a feeling of panic festering inside that was nothing to do with the screaming baby, or the horrible sick feeling. She didn't want to be left alone here, in this sumptuous house, with its sweeping views of sky and sea, not even with Colin and her mother. She didn't want Dad to take the car and drive back to Dublin without them, to start his painting. She was frightened, but she didn't know why.

Two people lay awake in Ballimagliesh that night. Father Hagan, looking out into the darkness over his tiny garden, said aloud, "Lord, Grant me a quiet night and a perfect end." Then he went to bed. But he didn't sleep. The faces of the new people at the Moynihan bungalow kept drifting into his mind and troubling him, the cousin's face particularly, with its flat white cheeks, its curious hard stare.

Mr Blakeman had set off for Dublin at seven that evening, when the baby had finally dropped off to sleep. But Prill didn't walk down the track with the others, to wave him goodbye as he turned the car out on to the metalled road. She shut herself in her room, flung herself down on the bed, and cried.

Chapter Three

COLIN WENT OUT before breakfast to have a look at the building site, and Oliver trailed after him. On the land side of the bungalow, where the earth sloped up and turned into a field, the builders had started digging a huge hole. There were piles of sand everywhere, and bricks stacked neatly. A yellow skip full of soil stood blocking the path to the back door.

"Do you think we could dig here?" Oliver said. "Are we allowed?"

It was the third time he'd asked Colin about what was "allowed". They had woken up early and decided to go out while the others slept on. "But are we *allowed*?" he'd asked anxiously, as Colin slid back the door bolts. "And are you allowed to go outside without your shoes on?" Aunt Phyllis must be very strict with him.

Colin looked at the piles of sand. "I shouldn't think it

would matter if you poked round here with a spade. When they come back in September they're going to dig down about three metres with an excavator. Well, so Dad said. The roof of the new garage will be level with the house, and it's going to be a patio with plants on, or something. It sounds very elaborate. What do you want to dig for, anyway?"

"I want to dig a hole," Oliver said, eyeing the shovels and spades propped against the concrete mixer.

"What on earth for?"

"I'd like to build a den."

"How babyish," Colin thought, and nearly said so. Then he thought better of it. After all, the best summer he could remember had been spent in a den, in a field behind their house, before they'd built the new estate. They had made it out of an enormous hole that used to be an air-raid shelter, roofed it over with bits of corrugated iron, and made a lookout with old tea-chests. It was the worst moment of his life when the contractors arrived, filling the hole in and flattening everything. He was just about Oliver's age then.

He said, "Well, I suppose it'd be all right. We'd better ask Dad though, when he rings up. You could always dig in the sand, Oliver. It looks a fabulous beach."

Oliver didn't reply. He'd never had a proper seaside holiday. He couldn't even swim. Those two had been going on in the car about swimming awards and different kinds of diving. He'd be happier up here on his own, digging his hole.

★ ★ ★

"That dog needs a long walk," Mum said after breakfast. Prill knew that voice, it was ragged at the edges. It meant she'd had enough of Alison bawling and of the others hanging around. She wanted some peace and quiet.

Jessie had spent a well-behaved night under the kitchen table but now she was tied up outside, barking madly at Kevin O'Malley, the boy from the farm who'd just brought them some milk.

"Come on," Prill said to Colin. "Let's take Jess down to the beach. Coming, Oliver?"

Colin waited for him to say no. He hoped his cousin would want to stay behind and make a start on his den. It would be a good chance for them to talk privately, and work out how they were going to survive for a month with him around. Colin wasn't very patient and Oliver was getting on his nerves. He hated the way he stared at people, and never spoke unless you spoke to him. Mum said that he was an only child, with rather elderly, fussy parents, and that they must "make allowances". But she didn't have to share a room with him.

"OK," Oliver said, quite eagerly. He put his anorak on and zipped it up.

"You don't need that, it's *boiling*!"

"I'm not hot."

He was already walking ahead of them, keeping well away from the dog as she leapt about wildly on the end of her lead. It was another perfect day and already very warm, but Prill felt better. A fresh smell of fields blew across as she followed

Chapter Three

Colin along the path, and the sick feeling had gone completely. Dad had phoned after breakfast to tell them he was making a start on his first sketches for the portrait. Yesterday's panic, down on the beach, seemed slightly ridiculous now.

"Not *that* way, Oliver," Colin was shouting. "We've got to drop down here, on to the shore. Come on." But Oliver carried on making for the green thicket that hid Donal Morrissey's caravan. "There's a footpath here," he shouted back. "I found it on a map."

"Oh, come on, can't you? We've been told that the old man... Oh, *damn!*" With an almighty tug, Jessie had wrenched the lead out of his hand and was tearing after Oliver, barking madly. The small boy started to run and soon disappeared into the trees. Colin and Prill pelted after him. Seconds later all three were standing at the open door of a decrepit wooden caravan. Colin had grabbed Jessie's collar and was trying to calm her down. Inches away, a mangy black collie, stretched out across the ramshackle steps, was growling at them.

"Be quiet, girl. *Sit!*" Colin shouted, but Jessie was almost throttling herself in her efforts to break free. The collie stood up, cringing and whining, then it took a step forward and showed its teeth. Bedlam followed. The two dogs made for each other in a tangle of hair, tongues, and frenzied barking. Oliver backed away and clutched nervously at Prill's arm. "Sit, can't you, *sit!* Gedoff, will you!" Colin was bellowing, and in the racket someone appeared in the doorway.

Donal Morrissey was thin and extremely tall, and stood glowering at them, his knotted hands shaking. The wispy remains of his hair blew about in the wind, silver-white but still reddish at the edges, and his bald, domed head was splodged with big freckles. He must once have had auburn hair, like Colin and me, thought Prill.

His face was so wrinkled it looked like a piece of paper someone had screwed up very tight then smoothed out again, leaving hundreds of tiny lines. There was so little flesh on it the skin was stretched over the bones like thin rubber, and every single one poked out. It was the kind of face you see in religious paintings.

But the voice that came from it was shrill and harsh. They couldn't tell whether he was speaking Irish or just making horrible noises at them to scare them off. They backed away as he came down the steps, waving his arms about and yelling.

Prill's stomach heaved. The old man stank. It was the smell of someone who never washed his hair, or his clothes, or had a bath. How could that Father Hagan come visiting him here, week after week? She'd be sick.

His dog had slunk off and was lying under the van, peering out at them. "Go on! Go on!" he was shouting. "There's been enough of it, I'm telling you. Leave a soul in peace will you, coming round here. God help me."

Jessie, always slow on the uptake, leapt at the old man and tried to lick his face. He lost his balance, swayed about, then fell heavily, crashing back against the side of the caravan. Prill gasped, he was so old, and Colin let go of Jessie and went to help him. But he was back on his feet almost at once, towering over them and letting out a stream of foul Irish as he pushed them back down the path, spitting the words out and slavering, his parchment cheeks turning a slow, bright red with pure rage.

As they reached the trees he picked up a handful of stones and flung them hard. Half a brick followed. There was nothing wrong with his eyesight. It caught Jessie in the middle of the back and she yelped with pain.

"Serves you right," Colin told the dog angrily when they were safely out of sight. Prill had found a handkerchief, licked it, and was dabbing gingerly at the gash on Jessie's back. The dog whined and twisted away, flattening its ears and flopping down in the grass. It knew quite well it was in disgrace.

"Poor old thing. She was only being friendly. That old man's mad. It wasn't just gravel you know, it was a brick." She went on stroking Jessie.

"Well, we were warned," Colin pointed out. "He's obviously got a thing about strangers. The builders must have really upset him, then a great red setter comes out of the blue and knocks him flying. Dad's right about Jessie, she has got a screw loose."

"A dog like that should have been painfully destroyed at birth," Oliver said suddenly. There was a dreadful silence. Colin looked at him in disbelief and Prill's mouth dropped open.

"That's a cruel thing to say... a really terrible thing." She wanted to cry, and Colin felt like hitting him. The two children loved Jessie; she was their best friend.

"It's a joke… only a joke…" Oliver stammered. "It's what my father says sometimes, about really awful pupils, you know."

They could imagine. Uncle Stanley was a teacher too. According to Dad he had a dry, sarcastic sense of humour, and sometimes reduced the boys in his school to tears. Colin stood up and said firmly, "Come here, Jessie." The dog came, like a lamb, and he fastened the lead on.

"If it hadn't been for you it would never have happened," Prill said. "You knew perfectly well that wasn't the way down to the beach. You just wanted to spy on him. I'd have thought you'd have had enough of old people, living with them all the time."

"Oh, let's get moving," Colin snapped. "I want a swim."

They set off down the track, but Oliver stayed where he was, staring after them.

"Hurry up, can't you?"

"I'm not coming. I'm going back to the bungalow."

"Mum did say we had to keep an eye on him," Prill whispered, then she shouted back, "Oh, come on, Oll, don't sulk."

"I'm not sulking."

"Leave him," Colin said impatiently. "Even he can't get lost between here and the house. We'll have a better morning without him, anyway."

Chapter Three

Oliver had no intention of going home. As soon as the other two had dropped out of sight he walked quickly back along the path, into the trees. His watch said twelve noon, the time the old man went for his daily drink at Danny's Bar in Ballimagliesh. He'd heard that priest telling Uncle David. "Never misses a day, regular as clockwork," he'd said.

From his hiding place he watched Donal Morrissey leave the van and walk off up the field with his dog at his heels. He moved quite quickly for such an old man, his hands thrust deep into the pockets of a ragged overcoat, a squashed green hat on his head. Oliver could hear him muttering as he walked past the neat little pyramids of peat blocks, stacked up to dry all along the track.

When he was out of sight the boy crept out and went up to the van. He pushed at the door and it swung inwards slowly. Oliver went in.

It was dark and hot inside the caravan, and very smelly. He detected a dog, and dirty clothes, and food that should have been thrown away. Something else too, a sharp scent, slightly sweet, the peat the old man was burning on his stove. Mother had said you never forgot the smell of it. She'd lived in Ireland once.

In the middle of the floor was a table, a chair, and a filthy dog blanket. All round him cardboard cartons were stacked up to the roof, and he could see junk heaped in corners, broken furniture and bags of rubbish, old biscuit tins, rusty tools. It looked like a rag-and-bone man's yard.

The mess didn't surprise Oliver. At home his favourite

resident, Mr Catchpole, lived in a room just like this, with a kind of nest in the middle for his bed and television set. Everywhere else was stuffed with rubbish, except that Oliver and Mr Catchpole knew it wasn't rubbish. It was the story of his life. All his eighty-three years were stacked up in boxes in that bedroom on the second floor. Memories mattered to old people, that's why they kept things.

The smell in the van was making him feel ill. He was dying to have a look in the biscuit tins but he felt queasy, so he climbed down the van steps again and took a few breaths of fresh air.

On the sea side of the van there was a tiny patch of garden. The neat rows of vegetables were a strange contrast with the mess inside. Perhaps someone from the farm helped him. According to that priest, the O'Malleys thought a lot of Donal Morrissey. He had worked for the family for years and years.

Suddenly Oliver noticed something moving on the bright green potato leaves and bent down for a closer look. One of the plants was a mass of small stripy insects. He felt in his pocket for his little magnifying glass then remembered he'd left it in the bedroom. But he did have a matchbox. Very carefully he picked a couple of the beetles off a leaf and shut them inside.

He walked up and down the rows of vegetables stopping to turn leaves over and inspect the stalks. Something was attacking Donal Morrissey's potato crop. The striped creatures had eaten great holes in the leaves, and what remained was covered with dark pink grubs. There would be tens of thousands by the end of the summer, unless something was done about it.

When he stood up again he spotted someone waving at him a couple of fields away. It was Kevin O'Malley, the curly-haired boy from the farm who'd brought the milk that morning. He'd tell him about it. He might know about spraying crops.

Then he thought better of it. This was something he could tackle on his own. He knew quite a bit about natural history from his father, more than those Blakemans, with their swimming and their athletics. They thought he was weedy anyway. And he didn't like the way they'd talked about the old man; Prill had said he was mad.

Oliver suddenly thought of something. He knelt down again, gritted his teeth, and grasped one of the plants hard, shaking off the insects as they ran over his fingers. He pulled it out of the earth. It wasn't exactly stealing, all that came out of the ground were some shrivelled skins, a bit like large raisins. Poor Donal Morrissey.

Kevin O'Malley waved again, and shouted something, but Oliver pretended not to hear. He slipped the matchbox into his pocket and, holding the potato plant at arm's length, started to walk rapidly in the direction of the bungalow.

Chapter Four

COLIN WOKE UP and clicked his light on. It was two in the morning. Oliver slept peacefully in the other bed, his warm pyjamas buttoned right up to the neck. But his face looked cool.

Colin was red hot. He wore nothing but thin cotton trousers and these, like his bedding, were soaked with sweat. He felt unwell, horribly warm and rather dizzy, and there were griping pains in his stomach, like the pangs of hunger, though he'd had a big meal quite late in the evening.

Prill was right, there was a funny smell about this place. She had told him about it that morning, how she'd gone along the beach looking for a dead animal, the stench was so overpowering.

Colin had been doubtful. Prill did sometimes get odd ideas into her head. She had a wild imagination. Now and then her English compositions were quite fantastic. He was more down to earth. "Uninspired" was usually scrawled across his essay.

"What kind of smell?" he'd wanted to know.

"Rich, but sickly. Rotten, yet sweet somehow. It really turned my stomach."

"Was it like pigs?"

They both laughed at this. Dad had once booked a country holiday for them in a bed and breakfast place that had turned out to be a pig farm. Pigs had a very strong, sweetish smell, a bit like sugar boiling, a bit like hops in a brewery. They'd all smelt of pigs, all holiday.

The bedroom window had been stuck fast with paint, and Dad had prised it open with a screwdriver. But now Colin shut it again, anything to get rid of that smell. If it was fertiliser they'd used an awful lot of it. Perhaps the O'Malleys were making up for lost time, with Dr Moynihan's money.

He sat down again, his head swimming; the foul smell was still there, though fainter. He felt himself falling forwards and put his hands out flat, to steady himself. The bedclothes were sodden. He stood up and felt them; pillows, sheets and stripy cover were all very damp, almost wet. The sweat of one boy couldn't have caused all that.

And there was something else. At the risk of waking Oliver he switched the main light on. He had to be sure. Mixed with the farmyard smell there was a mustiness in the room that reminded him of a cellar, and it was coming from his bed. Then he saw why. The edges of his sheets and pillowcase were softly edged with grey, and a greenish fuzz was starting to form in patches over them.

He put out a shaky hand and touched it. The cobwebby strands fell away and became a green cloud, dispersing slowly into the clammy air. It was decay.

Just for a second Colin felt like screaming. Some strange atmospheric condition must be causing all this heat and stench, making a mould form on everything in the room. What he needed was a gust of cold fresh air. He ought to fling the windows wide open, but he just couldn't bear that smell from the fields.

At least he could open the door. He stumbled past Oliver's bed and stubbed his toe on something hard. The sudden pain made him plump down abruptly on to the carpet. His cousin turned over, muttered a jumble of words, but slept on. Colin pulled out something that Oliver had been trying to hide with his bedspread. It was a large glass bottle, the kind used for making home-brewed beer; Mum had discovered six of them at the back of a kitchen cupboard. Oliver had filled the bottle with green leaves, already chewed to tatters by some striped insects that were crawling about inside. There were dozens of them.

Colin didn't like beetles much. He noticed with relief that the top of the container was firmly corked and sealed, but in a way the mad activity of the tiny creatures gorging on potato plants in the middle of the night made him feel less panic-stricken. So this was what Oliver had been up to in the afternoon, creeping around secretively, even more silent than usual, shutting himself up in the bedroom with his insect books. What on earth was he playing at?

His face was very close to Oliver's bedspread. It too felt damp. There was no sign of the green must he'd found in his half of the room, but he could still smell the mouldiness, mixed up with that sickening rotten smell.

He knew he would be awake till daylight came so he opened the door and lay down flat on the strip of carpet between the beds, taking slow, deep breaths, trying desperately to calm himself. Having the door open made no difference at all. Heat hit him in the face like the sting of boiling water. He lay there in panic, hating everyone in the house for being fast asleep.

Prill was asleep, but dreaming. The small green field that sloped away from her window had turned into a vast sweep of dark earth and it was raining. She knew it was autumn, from the trees.

In the distance someone was moving about, not walking upright but crawling over the soil, like an animal trying to reach its hole. In the dream Prill didn't move, but suddenly the scene was jerked nearer and she could see everything clearly, right up against her face. The field was planted with some crop that was rotting as it grew. The stalks were bright green but the leaves had turned slimy and dark. The whole field was black, as if a fire had swept over it.

The crawling figure was a woman, with arms and legs like sticks. She moved painfully, rooting among the scorched leaves, clawing at the soil, putting what looked like clods of earth into her mouth then spewing them out on to the slime of the furrows.

Prill closed her eyes, willing the picture to go away, but when she opened them the woman was outside the window, her mouth open in a scream and the wet soil dripping out of it. Her ridged yellow fingernails plucked at the pane, and Prill saw her face, with its high, domed forehead, its cloud of reddish hair, the prominent cheeks from which all the flesh had dropped away.

She was crying out, but Prill heard nothing. She was helpless, cut off, sealed away behind a thick wall of glass through which the woman moved and implored her, bobbing and jerking about like some ghastly marionette.

She shouted in her sleep and woke up suddenly. She was out of bed and standing by the open window breathing in great lungfuls of air. It was getting light. The small green field was misty, the air fresh and cool. The countryside and sea were very peaceful in the early dawn.

In the quietness she heard a light click on and then the baby started crying. She had been yelling on and off all night. Prill went down the hall to the kitchen and found Colin there, talking to his mother. He wore nothing except his blue pyjama trousers and his face looked hot. Mum had just stuck a thermometer into his mouth. She looked relieved to see Prill.

"Oh, hello, love. So you couldn't sleep either. Now we're all awake, except Oliver. I'll have to get a doctor to look at

Alison. She's only had about two hours' sleep all night. Just look at her."

She looked. The baby wasn't pink, like Colin, she was turkey red and her whole body was tense. Prill picked her up and tried to slip a finger into the tiny hand; she loved it when the little fingers curled tightly round her own. But Alison wouldn't respond. Both her hands were clenched up into hard little knots, and she was wailing.

"Has she been eating?"

"Yes. That's what I don't understand. It's not as if she's hungry. How can she be?"

"Perhaps she's got what I've got," Colin mumbled, removing the thermometer and reading it. "I feel most odd. Oh, that's funny. My temperature's not up, Mum."

The electric kettle clicked off. "Let's have some tea," Mrs Blakeman said wearily. "When in doubt have a cup of tea." She was trying to sound cheerful but Prill wasn't fooled, she looked so tired and strained, not a bit like her usual self. She didn't panic easily. "Do you think Oliver would like some?"

"Oh, he's still dead to the world," Colin said. "I should think he's the only one who's had a good night's sleep, lucky devil!"

Prill took the milk jug out of the fridge. The smell made her wrinkle her nose up. "*Ugh!* We can't use this, Mum. It's off."

"It can't be. The O'Malley boy brought it straight up from their dairy. It was chilled. Anyway, I used it at supper, Oliver had some Ovaltine."

"Well, it's off *now*."

Colin took the large brown jug and sniffed, then he carried it to the sink and looked more closely under the electric strip light. The contents of the jug had solidified completely, they were now greyish, and a fine hair was forming on the thick, wrinkled skin.

He upturned the jug into the sink and a slimy gel plopped out on to the stainless steel. There was a sharp, bitter smell.

"It must be the fridge," Mum said, more concerned about the whimpering baby. "Perhaps there's a lemon. We could have that with our tea."

"The fridge light's on," Colin said numbly. "And the motor's going, listen. It's working all right." In the quietness they could hear the motor humming gently.

"This fridge is brand new," Prill pointed out. "Look, they've not even taken the label off it."

Colin carefully washed the stinking mess down the sink. Prill came up and looked over his shoulder. "I wish Dad was here," he muttered, out of the side of his mouth so Mrs Blakeman couldn't hear him. "I think Alison looks awful."

Prill was trying to convince herself that the woman outside the window had been a nightmare. She did not succeed, no more than Colin succeeded in persuading himself that he'd imagined that fuzzy growth on his pillow.

"It's this house," she whispered back. "I wish we'd never come."

Chapter Five

BUT AS THE earth warmed up and birds started singing, Alison, exhausted by her night's bawling, fell asleep abruptly in her mother's arms. Mum crept to the kitchen door and mouthed, "I'm going back to bed for a bit."

"Good idea. I'm going too," Prill told Colin. "I feel as if I've been awake all night." She was thinking, Dad'll be phoning at ten o'clock and I'm going to ask him to come back. I can't bear it here.

Colin sat in the kitchen for a few minutes, looking out over the sea. He felt quite cold suddenly, but it was going to be another beautiful day. There wasn't a cloud in sight and the stillness in the air promised another scorcher. He still had hunger pains so he made himself some toast and another mug of lemon tea. Then he found the sleeping bag that Dad had stuffed under the stairs, unrolled it over the damp mattress and fell soundly asleep.

At eight o'clock they were all still sleeping, except Oliver. He got up at seven, dressed stealthily, and crept round the kitchen looking for something to eat. Jessie whined and nosed at his feet. He refilled her bowl with fresh water, holding it at arm's length in case she bit him. He was frightened of dogs. Then he went outside, selected a spade, and started to dig his hole. His uncle David had told Colin on the phone that he was allowed to dig, provided he left the earth in a tidy pile.

The other two didn't get up again till half past ten and by then Colin was ravenous. He sat at the kitchen table eating cornflakes, toast, eggs and bacon. All the windows were wide open. They could hear Oliver scraping away at his hole and talking to Kevin O'Malley who'd walked down with the milk. Mixed with the smell of fields was the tang of the sea.

"There's not much wrong with *you*," Prill said. "I don't know how you can eat all that."

"I was hungry," Colin said simply. "It woke me up in the night."

"Was that all that woke you?"

"What do you mean?"

"Well, you were in the kitchen at five o'clock."

"So were you."

They stared at each other, Prill with a look that said, "You first". Colin pressed his lips together. Prill was nervous sometimes. When they were little he used to get into awful rows for jumping out at her and making spooky noises. She still slept with the landing light on.

"What was the matter?" she asked him.

He hesitated.

"Come on, Colin!" her voice was strained, almost angry. It wasn't like Prill. He was supposed to be the moody one.

"Well, it sounds so stupid… It was weird. I woke up because I was too hot, and my bed felt terribly damp, and… there was a kind of, well, mould all over it."

"*Mould?*"

"Yes, honestly, and it smelt peculiar too, horribly musty."

She stood up. "Show it to me."

"It's no good, Prill, not now. Sit down, will you? I can't. It wasn't there when I woke up just now. Everything had, well, you know, gone back to normal. The sheets are a bit dirty, that's all. I was probably dreaming."

She was silent. A wave of fear rose inside her then ebbed away, leaving her numb and cold. "That makes it worse," she said.

"What do you mean?"

"The fact that it's all so…ordinary this morning. It's like that smell on the beach. It *was* there. But you just said I must have imagined it."

"You didn't imagine it. I could smell it too, last night. I was nearly sick." He paused. "What woke you up, the same thing?"

"No… *no*. It was Alison, yelling her head off. Then, when I did get to sleep, I had a kind of nightmare. It was about Donal Morrissey but he'd, sort of, turned into a woman. She looked more like a skeleton. Ugh, it was horrible."

She wouldn't say any more. Shaking her head violently, as if this would shatter the picture in her mind of the woman crawling over the field, she went to the wall-phone and started dialling.

"What are you doing?"

"Phoning Dad."

"Why?"

"I want to talk to him."

"But he'll ring us, before he starts painting. You know that's the arrangement."

"Well, it's gone eleven and he's not phoned yet." She put the receiver to her ear and listened.

"Is it ringing at the exchange? They'll take ages to answer."

"No," she said flatly. "And it isn't going to ring either. It's completely dead. No wonder Dad can't get through."

Oliver had marked out where he was going to dig with four sticks and tied string at each corner. He hadn't got down very far because he kept finding things. His treasures were neatly arranged on a plastic tray he'd found in the kitchen. Prill sat outside miserably and fingered them. There were some pieces of china, a halfpence piece, and several bits of white tubing with holes through them.

"What are these, Oliver?"

"Bits of a clay pipe, I should think."

He went on digging, puffing in the heat; he was still

wearing a long-sleeved sweater even though it was seventy degrees and getting hotter.

"Why don't you wash the soil off?"

He leaned on his spade like a little old man and said witheringly, "You don't wash things like this, Prill, they might disintegrate. That's what the toothbrush is for. You have to brush the dirt off very gently."

Although Oliver was scraggy and small there was something very adult about him. Prill didn't like the look in those large blue eyes of his. It said so plainly that he thought she was both ignorant and stupid.

He was the only person who didn't seem affected by the house. She and Colin had talked about that in the kitchen. Nothing had made Oliver wake up in the night sweating, there had been no mould or mustiness round him. And he certainly hadn't complained about a smell; the only smell he didn't like was Alison when she needed a fresh nappy. In fact, the baby seemed to upset him rather a lot, especially when she cried. Prill had seen him actually put his fingers in his ears when he thought nobody was looking.

"Well, he's used to being on his own at home," Mum had said. "And he's been ill, don't forget. He was in bed for weeks, and Auntie Phyl kept him very quiet. Anyway, a din like that might get on your nerves too if all you'd ever been used to was a house full of old people." But Prill still felt like thumping him.

Colin and his mother had gone with Alison on a walk up to the O'Malleys' farm. Jessie went with them, mad with delight at being released from the concrete mixer. Mrs O'Malley rang the exchange to tell them the bungalow phone wasn't working. "It's funny that," she said. "All the phones go off together usually, when we have gales. But last night was calm enough. Still, they'll come to it to be sure, eventually. You didn't need it today, did you?"

"No-o," Mrs Blakeman said slowly. "Though my husband will have been trying to get through, and I had just wondered about getting a doctor to look at the baby. She's been really miserable since we got here."

The farmer's wife took Alison on her lap. The baby gurgled and grabbed at the strings of her apron. "She looks grand now, a real grand girl she is. Oh, that's bold!" And she prised Alison's fingers away from the chain round her neck.

"I think it must be the weather," Mum said. "We've all been terribly hot. We are expecting it to rain all the time."

Mrs O'Malley looked puzzled. "It's not been so hot, has it?" Then she smiled. "I've been so busy lately, I've probably just not noticed."

"Our milk went off last night," Colin said suddenly. His mother frowned at him. "I left it out after supper," she said firmly. "I must have, and obviously the heat turned it."

Kevin appeared in the kitchen doorway and started pulling his boots off. "Don't do that," his mother ordered. "Slip across to the dairy and fetch some more milk for Mrs Blakeman. Last night's was off apparently."

Mum was embarrassed. "Really," she began. "We really don't need—"

Chapter Five

"Don't worry about it, Mrs Blakeman. It may well have been the old milk you got, by mistake. It happens sometimes. I'll ask Donal. He helps us in the evenings and he gets confused these days about what goes where."

Kevin came back with a can and put it on the table. He grinned at Colin. "I've been trying to persuade your cousin to go up the Yellow Tunnel, but he doesn't seem too keen. He wants to keep on with his digging."

"What's the Yellow Tunnel?"

"Well, if you want a good walk, one that'll tire out that dog of yours, go along the shore, below the bungalow. You could do it this afternoon, it's low tide. You walk right along the sands as far as Ballimagliesh Strand then you can climb up to the chapel. It's a ruin really, right on the cliff edge. It's a proper beauty spot, isn't it, Mam?"

"So it is. We used to have picnics there years ago. All the young people went. Beautiful, it is."

"But what about this tunnel?"

"Well, there's a track up to the ruin, through the grass, a bit steep in places but sure it's fine in dry weather like this. But you *can* climb up through a crack in the rocks. It's great. It brings you out by the chapel walls in the middle of the old graveyard."

"Do you need ropes?"

"Oh no, there are plenty of footholes. But I should take a torch."

Colin could see that climbing up a real tunnel might not appeal to Oliver, and anyway, Mum might prefer him not to do it. He was still rather shaky after his illness. Digging a little hidey-hole in your garden was one thing, feeling your way up a great crack gouged out by the waves was quite another. It appealed to Colin, though.

When they were back at the bungalow he got everybody organized. Prill didn't need persuading. She cheered up a bit when he told her Mrs O'Malley had reported that their phone was out of order, but she still didn't want to stay in the house.

"Well, who wants to, anyway," Colin said, "on a day like this?"

They put some food together and installed Alison in a canvas carrier that Colin usually wore on his back like a rucksack. Most days she didn't care who carried her around but she was being awkward this morning. It had to be Mum.

Oliver kept on digging till the very last moment, muttering darkly that he didn't want to go. He had things to do that afternoon which didn't include the Blakemans.

"Oh, come on, Olly!" Prill shouted. "We're wasting the day. It'll be cooler down by the sea. You could take your sweater off," she added, unable to resist.

"I don't think—" he began.

"Look, it's only a bit of a climb up a cliff path. You can walk with Mum if the tunnel's bothering you. Don't be so pathetic," Colin said impatiently.

That did it. Oliver chucked his spade down, pushed past both of them, and was soon walking with Mrs Blakeman. It was quite peaceful. At least the carrier was keeping that awful baby quiet.

Chapter Six

As they walked along the beach, Oliver was planning his getaway. This was his sly streak coming out. He did have one, and he told lies sometimes to get what he wanted. He'd once listened, through a closed door, to his parents discussing the fact that he was adopted. "Perhaps it's not our fault," his father said. "Perhaps it's just, well, in the blood."

"Blood? Rubbish!" his mother had said sharply. "It's training. He's our son now and he'll tell the truth." That night he'd been made to stay in his room without anything to eat. Mother was very strict with him. Sometimes she seemed to forget he was just a little boy. Mr Catchpole was scared of her too.

It was a long walk to the Yellow Tunnel. In spite of its name, Ballimagliesh Strand seemed to be miles beyond the village. They could soon see the crumbly yellow cliffs that gave the crack its name, but it never seemed to get any nearer.

The dog leaped ahead and was soon out of sight. Oliver plodded along at his aunt's side. The sand and the sea, all bathed in sunshine, lifted everybody's spirits, but made no impact at all on him. His mind was full of beetles. Overnight the leaves in the jar had been virtually chewed to nothing, and he was certain the insects had multiplied. He must go back and talk to Donal Morrissey. *He* wasn't scared of him.

Gradually he dropped behind and left his aunt to walk on her own. Colin and Prill were deep in conversation, about him probably. He dropped back still farther and pretended to examine a bit of driftwood. Then, when the others were well ahead, and Mrs Blakeman nearly out of sight, he turned round and started to walk back.

Colin saw him. "What are you doing, Oliver? Get a move on."

"I think I'll go back."

"Why, for heaven's sake? It's not much farther now."

Oliver dithered. Words like "Too hot", "Not swimming" and "Doing a bit more to my hole" floated along the beach. He saw Prill take a step towards him then Colin holding her arm. "I can make the tea," he shouted. "Well, I can get the table ready and everything, for when you come back." He liked Auntie Jeannie and it might please her. That squalling baby was definitely getting on her nerves.

"Will you be all right on your own?" Prill called to him. She didn't sound so bad-tempered as Colin. "You don't have to climb the tunnel. You can go with Mum. Anyway, the bungalow's locked."

"I'll ask Mrs O'Malley to let me in. She's got a key. I'll be all right," he shouted. He was already turning his back, but he saw Colin pulling Prill impatiently in the other direction. "An utter drip" and "Chicken" were the last words he heard as he hurried along the beach, much faster now.

The door of Donal Morrissey's caravan was shut, but smoke poured from the tin chimney. Oliver crept up through the vegetable patch and examined the plants at his feet. The stripy beetles were still thriving and nibbling away steadily, turning the leaves into pieces of green lace.

He stood up, took a deep breath, and hammered on the door. Instantly a dog barked inside. Oliver quaked. He was scared of dogs and that collie was a brute. But there was no time to run. The door opened and Donal Morrissey was looking down at him, holding on to the growling dog with a bit of rope.

Their eyes met. The old man's gaze terrified Oliver. The wide-eyed, bloodshot stare was full of threat and there was an awful hardness about it. It was a face from which every drop of human kindness suddenly seemed to have drained away.

"What do you want? Get away from here or I'll set this dog on you. I told you yesterday." He gave the collie a bit more rope and it leaped to Oliver, snapping its teeth.

"I've come to—" he began nervously, taking a few steps back.

"Leave me alone, coming here with your noise. I'll get the Garda on to you! Leave an old man in peace can't you, in the name of God, or you'll be sorry for it!"

The door crashed shut in Oliver's face and the whole van shook. Inside, the dog went on barking and the old man shouted, a mumbled torrent of fast Irish of which the boy could make nothing, save the fact that he'd be wise to make a quick retreat before that dog was let loose and old Morrissey went off to find a policeman.

"I just came to tell you that your *vegetable patch* needs looking at, Mr Morrissey! It's got some kind of *infestation*! I know about insects, you see!" he shouted helpfully, from a safe distance. "If you don't do something your crop'll be ruined, that's all I came to say."

"Mother of God, will you get off my land!" came the strangled voice from inside, and through a filthy side window Oliver saw two bloody eyes staring out at him. "Don't be telling me how to farm. It's a count of ten I'm giving you to get out of my sight, and I'm starting now."

Through the yelps of the dog Oliver heard him chanting, "One, two, three…" It reminded him of hide and seek. In less than a minute he was hidden in the trees, well off Donal Morrissey's "land", that pathetic, wind-blown plot of poor soil, planted so lovingly, marooned in the middle of the O'Malleys' fields. You'd think it was a thousand acres, from his crazy behaviour.

But Oliver knew what he had to do. Old people had funny ideas sometimes, and they often got frightened when

Chapter Six

you were only trying to help them. Donal Morrissey was nearly ninety and wouldn't respond to common sense any more. Drastic measures were called for.

He went straight back to the bungalow. There was no need to bother Mrs O'Malley, he could let himself in with the spare key. It hung inside one of the kitchen cupboards and Oliver had pocketed it that morning. This was the kind of sneaky behaviour that made his mother angry. "He needs watching," she'd warned her niece Jeannie, when they were discussing the holiday. "Once that child gets an idea in his head there's *no stopping him.*" Mrs Blakeman had only half-listened. She liked Aunt Phyl but she did fuss over children.

As he got everything ready Oliver thought about his two cousins, shinning athletically up the walls of some ghastly tunnel. And he'd given them the slip. He grinned to himself as he stuffed matches into his anorak pocket and poked around in the utility room for the vital cans. He found them among paint pots and household cleaners and also a garden broom, propped in a corner. That might just be useful.

Before setting off he had a final look at his *Naturalist's Pocket Book*, then at the jar. The green plant the bugs were feeding on was starting to wilt and turn yellow. They would die soon.

He looked at Colin's bare mattress. The sheets and blankets lay on the floor in a grubby heap with the dog's pawmarks all over them. He'd said something about waking up in the night because the bed was damp and the room smelt musty, and he'd mentioned an awful smell outside.

Oliver couldn't understand it. Everything looked perfectly normal to him, and Colin was such a hard-headed, no-nonsense type, a bit like his own mother.

But those sheets weren't fit to sleep in. Oliver decided to be forgiving and to try and please everybody. He bundled them up, took them to the kitchen, and set the washing machine going. He knew exactly what to do. One of his jobs at home was putting the washing through. Then he went back to his bedroom and inspected the jar again. After a minute's hesitation he decided to take it with him. He picked it up and went outside. It was nearly half past four. With luck, Donal Morrissey would be on his way to the O'Malleys to help with the evening milking.

Before he struck his first match, Oliver checked and double checked. All the affected plants were thoroughly soaked and the two cans empty. It was so dry that what he had to do wouldn't take long. The leaves would catch and be scorched, the pests would perish, and anything worth eating could still be pulled up. He knew all about burning the fields at the end of summer; "swaling" it was called in Cheshire, where his father had been brought up on a farm.

The air was still. He'd checked that. They didn't burn the fields when a high wind was blowing. Carefully, but with a certain excitement, he slid open the matchbox.

Within seconds the whole of Donal Morrissey's vegetable patch was ablaze. Oliver stood by the caravan and watched it burning; there was much more smoke than he'd expected and the plants gave off a bitter smell that caught at his throat and made his eyes water. It was going well. Very soon the whole thing would be over. The old man would thank him for this in time; he was doing what Donal Morrissey couldn't or wouldn't do. He was cleansing the earth with fire.

He felt somehow triumphant. Without really thinking what he was doing, he unsealed the glass jar, pulled out the yellowing stalks and flung them into the flames. Then he shook the debris out from the bottom. The tiny, engorged creatures on the withered leaves disappeared into the smoke, spitting and crackling. Everything must be destroyed. Oliver stood back and surveyed his small fire with satisfaction.

Then his blood ran cold. There *was* a breeze. Not much of one, but it had sprung up from somewhere and was strong enough to bend the flames towards him. And while the vegetable patch was metres away from the van, there was something he'd not noticed before stacked against one end, a big pile of twigs for kindling. Peat was a slow burner, according to his mother; you always needed small stuff to get it going.

The heaped twigs had ignited and turned into a bonfire. Another little gust sent the flames licking along the underside of the van. One wheel caught fire and a window darkened with smoke. Then, from inside, a dog started barking.

In terror Oliver looked for the garden broom. There it was, at the end of the plot, propped against a post. But he couldn't reach it. The furrows were full of stubble and dry grass, all kinds of rubbish made bone dry by the hot weather, and everything was burning now with big flames. The intense heat drove Oliver back to the van and he saw fire nibbling along the underside, making a start on the wooden steps. The dog barked and whined and he heard it scratching pathetically on the inside of the door. He pulled at it but it was fastened with a rusty hasp and fixed with a padlock. Someone stronger could have prised it apart with a screwdriver, or bashed it in with a stone. But Oliver was too feeble. There was no stone, and the flames were scorching his shoes.

The boy screamed and stepped back. He tried to stamp on the flames then ripped off his anorak and beat at them with it, but it was useless, so he climbed on to a stinking dustbin then clawed his way up on to the roof itself. Tearing off his sweater and T-shirt he jumped up and down like a maniac, waving them madly, screaming for help, as the poor dog barked frantically inside and howled for release.

On Thursdays Donal didn't help with the milking. It was his night for a long drinking session at Danny's Bar. Most of his old friends were dead now, but he liked the crack. On the Ballimagliesh road he'd met Father Hagan and told him about his potatoes and what the boy had said. The priest was a gardener too.

"Will I walk back with you now, Donal, and give it a look over?" Father Hagan said gently, turning his bike round. The old man was going earlier and earlier to Danny's these days. "I'll drink a cup of tea with you, will I, then we'll see if John

O'Malley's got a spray you could use."

But they met the farmer in the yard and he walked up the fields with them. The farmhouse was sheltered by a sweep of land and had no views. Only after a long pull up the track could John O'Malley see most of his fields, the sea, and the old man's caravan. But long before they reached the brow of the hill he knew something was wrong. He could smell burning. A dog was squealing frantically and a child crying out like a tormented soul, screaming for help.

He dropped the spray-gun he was carrying and ran, and Father Hagan lumbered up the slope after him, leaving the old man on his own. The sudden effort made the priest wheeze and groan, but for such a large man he moved quickly. His jacket filled with wind and billowed and flapped round him like a big black flag.

The vegetable plot was still blazing strongly. Father Hagan grabbed the broom then dropped it again; the handle was red-hot and smouldering. He took his coat off and spread it on the flames, then trampled on it. John O'Malley picked up an old chisel from the rubbish round the van, wrenched the door open and the dog leaped out. It had chewed the rope to pieces in its terror. Somewhere inside the old man stored drinking water in a couple of buckets. The farmer lugged them through the door and threw the contents at the caravan wheels, then refilled them at an old rainwater barrel a little way down the track.

The fire hadn't really taken hold of the caravan, but he needed more help. "Leave that, Father, it'll burn itself out. This needs the water, I'm thinking. *You!*" he yelled up to Oliver. "Come down here, will you. Make a chain with Father Hagan."

Numb, but sagging with relief, Oliver slithered off the roof and staggered towards the water barrel on weak legs. The priest filled the first bucket, and Oliver carried it to John O'Malley who doused the flames under the van. One wheel and the steps were burning too fiercely to be saved, and to stop the fire spreading upwards the farmer brought out a rusty axe from inside and chopped them away, leaving them to burn themselves out on the scorched earth.

The bonfire of kindling wood was still flaring wildly. Bucket after bucket of water was hurled over it and eventually a thick white cloud enveloped the caravan, shrouding everything but the tin chimney.

The old man reached the brow of the hill alone and stared down at the fire. From where he stood the flames were still quite high and his home wreathed in smoke. The dog yapped and whined at his feet and tried to get under his coat. "Husht now, husht," he whispered to it, gathering it into his arms like a baby. Then the breeze wafted another noise up to him, the terrified sobbing of a child.

Old memories stirred in Donal Morrissey then. He gazed numbly at the scene at the end of the track, his home in flames, the men going to and fro with buckets, the boy helplessly crying. Tears ran down his crumpled face and made dark splashes on the earth.

Chapter Seven

THE CHAPEL RUIN was the most peaceful place Prill had ever been in. She never forgot those last few moments of darkness, scrambling up after Colin and his bobbing ring of torchlight, then bursting up into the sunshine and flinging herself down on soft grass.

Perhaps it was sheer relief. She hadn't liked the tunnel much, it was much longer and harder to climb than Kevin O'Malley had made out. But it fascinated Colin. He couldn't wait to come back and have another look with a better flashlight. "We might find something really interesting in there," he said as he fished about in the picnic basket for something to eat. "Next time we'll—"

"We'll *nothing*," Prill said. "Include me out, anyway. The Ballimagliesh kids have been coming here for donkey's years, according to Kevin's mother. Didn't you see all the sweet papers and the initials carved on the walls? Shouldn't think there's anything much in there."

Mrs Blakeman had taken the grassy, zigzag path up on to the headland and was waiting anxiously for them. She looked most relieved when their dirty faces popped up out of the crack. Alison was bawling again.

"It's no good," she said, only half-listening to Colin's raptures about the tunnel and Prill's explanation about Oliver going back. "I'm taking this child to the doctor's tomorrow, there *is* something wrong with her. She's only happy when she's asleep. The minute she woke up she started yelling. She's usually so good-tempered."

Colin lifted the wriggling baby out of the canvas carrier and dumped her on the grass. She couldn't walk yet but she was a demon crawler. "Watch her, Mum," he warned. "She'll be down that hole in a minute."

Mrs Blakeman picked her up and walked over to the main ruin with Prill. Nothing was left of the chapel but a few low walls of crumbling stone and one massive arch that must have held a window. You could still see the delicate tracery on the great columns at each side. Through the arch the sea glittered. Apart from Alison's constant grizzling everything was very quiet. In the long grass, where the main aisle must have been, was a pool of clear water.

"How odd," Prill said, trailing her hand in. "There's a kind of spring here. But it must have been right in the middle of the church."

"It was, according to that priest who dropped in on us,

that Father Hagan. It was their local miracle or something, hundreds of years ago, in a drought, he said. It was the only water for miles around."

"Wonder why they deserted it?"

"Oh, places do fall into disuse. I suppose it happened when they built a new church in Ballimagliesh."

"Those graves must be ancient," Prill said, looking across at Colin who was scraping away with his penknife at something in the grass. The leaning tombstones had been eaten away by years of mild, wet weather into strange mossy lumps. Lichens had woven themselves across in silent trellises of yellow-green and burnt orange. Words that had once proclaimed names and dates and manners of death had mouldered away, and only tantalizing fragments of odd letters remained.

But though the dead lay all around them Prill didn't want to go back to the bungalow. She felt safer out here. "Do we have to go back now, Mum?" she said as her mother manoeuvred the baby back into the sling, which was now on Colin's back. "No, *no*, Alison," she was saying snappily. "Stay with Colin now. Colin's going to carry you home." The baby tried to stand up in the sling and grabbed at her mother's hair. Mrs Blakeman stuffed the arm back quite roughly and the child howled.

Prill was amazed. Her mother must be really worried. She decided she had better take charge of the dog and stop moaning about going back. She called her over but Jessie was drinking noisily at the little pool and just wagged her tail cheekily. At last she persuaded her to come away and together they followed Mrs Blakeman down the cliff path. Colin, with the baby on his back, was trying to bend down and have a final squint at the headstone he'd found half buried in the grass.

Mum was already well ahead. "Oh, come *on*, Colin!" she shouted. "Leave it, whatever it is. This is the quickest route back, not so pretty as the way we came, but I *must* phone a doctor, and we'd better find out what Oliver's up to."

"Hope he's OK," Colin said thoughtfully, catching up with Prill. "Wonder how his hole's getting on?"

"He said he'd get our tea," Prill reminded him. "Some hope."

"I've got hunger pains," Colin said suddenly, putting one hand across his stomach. "Hope it's something good."

"You can't be hungry now," Prill said in disgust. "You've just eaten an apple and a great hunk of cake. You're just greedy. You'll get fat."

"Leave him alone, Prill," Mrs Blakeman shouted. "And stop dawdling. I want to get back. You really shouldn't have let Oliver go home, you know."

She was worrying now, not just about the baby but about him too. The boy was her responsibility and he wasn't very strong. That long spell of illness couldn't have improved his health. She'd told them to keep an eye on him. She didn't want to get back and find he'd collapsed or something.

It was only when they reached the crack at the bottom of the cliff that she discovered he'd been left behind.

Chapter Seven

"That boy needs watching!" rang and repeated in her head like a gong. She walked ahead of the two children, trying to shake off a steadily growing anxiety. Nothing was really going right on this holiday, in spite of the marvellously equipped bungalow and its glorious setting. The baby was ill and the other two had complained of feeling unwell. Oliver didn't seem to approve of anything or anybody. And it was much too hot. The moist, sticky atmosphere was becoming unbearable. Something was wrong, with everything.

When they were about half a mile from the bungalow they met Kevin O'Malley on the cliff path. Under the thatch of dark curly hair his usually reddish face was very pale.

"Mrs Blakeman," he began uncertainly. "Mam says will you come up to the house? There's been an accident."

"Oh God no, *Oliver!*" Her voice was a harsh shriek. The sheer helplessness in it, out of all proportion to what the boy had said, frightened Colin and Prill. It was so unlike their mother. Kevin put out his hand awkwardly. "No, missus, he's all right, only there was a bit of a blaze you see, in Morrissey's field. His van nearly went up, and the boy was there. If you could just come…"

"What on earth made you do it, love?" Mum whispered, taking a cup of tea from Mrs O'Malley. She had to say something, though Oliver's face was all red and puffy from crying. "If you really thought the old man's vegetables needed looking at you only had to—" then Mrs O'Malley shook her head and frowned. They'd been through all that once.

The farmer sat at the kitchen table brooding over his tea. He was a short, stocky man with curly hair like Kevin and a permanently anxious look. He was very grave.

"Y'see, missus," he said quietly, "Oliver here thought it was for the best. He thought Donal's crop had got the potato beetle and that burning the tops off was the surest way to get rid of it."

"I tried to tell him," sniffed Oliver. "He just wouldn't listen."

"I don't know if the boy was right. There's nothing left of the plants. It's a pity you emptied your jar on to the fire, Oliver. I'll have to report this, you see. I could have shown it to them. Everyone round here will have to be told and put on the alert now. We do get pests from time to time, of course; farmers have to be on the lookout for them. But *potato beetle*, well that's more or less a thing of the past with all the modern pesticides. But of course it's no laughing matter. Let's hope you were mistaken, anyway."

"They weren't just… big ladybirds, were they, Oll?" Prill said. She was only trying to be helpful.

"*No*," he said, with a look of withering scorn. "I know what a ladybird looks like, you know." And Colin knew they weren't ladybirds, he'd seen them feasting on green leaves in the middle of the night. But he said nothing.

There was an embarrassing silence, broken only by Oliver's sniffing.

"You see, Oliver," Mum began again. "What you did was so dangerous, so drastic."

Chapter Seven

"It had to be drastic," he said, his voice suddenly quite firm again. "Drastic things need drastic cures sometimes." He sounded like a headmaster.

"What do you mean?"

"My father told me all about Ireland, before we came; there was a time when the people went hungry, a million starved to death, they say, because of the bad potato harvests."

John O'Malley looked across at him and his face cleared with sudden understanding. "You're right, Oliver, they did suffer, back in the 1840s, all over Europe, and it was at its worst here in Ireland. But it wasn't beetle, boy, it was blight. Oh, people still look out for it, even today. Sure, it was a terrible curse."

"What's blight?"

"Something carried in the air — tiny spores. It attacked the plants and made them go bad, whole fields went rotten, overnight virtually." He loosened his collar. "Weather like this'd be perfect for it, hot, and a bit sticky. Oh, we think we have a hard time on a tiny farm like this, but I'm telling you, we don't know we're born."

Nobody said anything, there was such passion in his voice. Sensing the embarrassment, he went on uncertainly. "Perhaps you know all about it anyway, from your history lessons? The Hungry Forties it was called."

"No," Prill said. "We've only reached the Normans." It sounded so pathetic.

"Old Donal's the one to ask about what went on round here," Mrs O'Malley said. "He knows a fair bit of history. He was quite a scholar in his day and he's got all kinds of bits and pieces in that van of his. You'll have to ask him to show you."

"I don't suppose he'll ever want to speak to *me* again," Oliver said bleakly. He wanted him to, somehow.

"He will, he will to be sure. Just give him a bit of time. He's kind enough, underneath, but he's had a bit of a shock… and we all get old."

"Where's he gone?" asked Oliver.

"He's staying with Father Hagan tonight. He'll be making him have a bath, if I know anything."

"I'll pay for the van," the boy said solemnly. "Whatever it costs, I'll pay. I'll… I'll write to my mother and ask her to send me the money, then I'll save up and pay her back."

It would take him years. His father was very stingy about pocket money. "No, Oliver," Mrs Blakeman said emphatically. "Don't worry your mother." She could just see Aunt Phyl coming out on the next boat. "We'll sort it out. Don't you worry about it. *And that's an order!*" And she smiled at him.

The atmosphere was easing slightly. "Did anyone come to the telephone?" Mrs Blakeman asked.

"Yes, missus, you were in luck, and it's been put right for you. I let them in," Kevin replied.

"Thank goodness for that. I want to speak to a doctor, Mrs O'Malley. I really don't think Alison's too well."

The farmer's wife looked at the baby. For once she was quiet and sitting pudding-like on Mrs Blakeman's lap. "Hmm. She's a bit flushed, I suppose." She plucked gently at the tiny wrist. "They always say thin babies are healthier. I wouldn't know about that. All mine were little barrels."

"*Thin?* But she's not *thin*, Mrs O'Malley? Well, I wouldn't say so." She sounded quite alarmed. Prill looked at Alison. She did look thinner, the little bracelets of fat on her wrists weren't quite so pudgy now, and her hands no longer looked like little paws. Only her face was fat-looking and it was swollen with heat and constant grizzling.

Mrs O'Malley realized she'd said the wrong thing. "Now don't you worry yourself, Mrs Blakeman, I'll ring Dr O'Keefe myself. He's grand. He'll be down to see you first thing tomorrow, if I know him. Now, how about something to eat for all of you? It's a long time since you ate, I'm thinking."

"Oh no, thank you." Mrs Blakeman got up abruptly. She looked distracted. "No, we've got food at the house. It's not fair to wish another brood upon you. The cup of tea was lovely but we'll get back now. Colin, can you get Jessie? Come on, Oliver." All she wanted was to get back to the bungalow and speak to her husband. Thank God they'd mended the phone.

The four of them walked slowly up the track in complete silence. The weather was changing, the sky was yellowish and the moist air stickier than ever. There were mutterings of thunder over the sea.

"We're in for a storm," Colin said.

"Good," Prill muttered. "We could do with some rain."

She reached the front door first and Mum handed her the key. She pushed it into the lock but could hardly bring herself to turn it. The key had become a lead lump, impossible to move, so desperately did she not want to enter that house.

"Hurry up, can't you?" Colin badgered impatiently.

Fighting tears back, wanting to run a million miles away, she pushed the door open slowly.

Chapter Eight

A CARD FROM the telephone engineer lay on the small table in the hall. Mum read it. "Thank goodness for that, I'll phone Dad in a minute."

"I'll get the exchange for you, shall I?" Prill said, pushing past the two boys and going into the kitchen. *It had to be now.* She picked the receiver up and listened, then she jiggled the black buttons up and down.

"It's not working."

Colin came up behind her, grabbed the phone and listened for himself. "That's ridiculous. This card says, 'An engineer called today as requested and we are pleased to inform you that—'"

"Oh, shut up, will you? It's just like it was before. It's as dead as a dodo." She went off to tell her mother.

"Why don't we use the O'Malleys' phone? Can I come

67

with you? We could go now."

"No-o, Prill," Mrs Blakeman said slowly. "They must have had enough of us for one day, after Oliver's performance with the petrol." Then something made her turn round. He was standing in the bedroom doorway in his pyjamas.

"That was quick. Don't you want any supper?"

"No. I just want to go to bed." His face was smeary from crying.

"All right, love, sleep well then. Do you think you should send your mother a card in the morning, just to tell her you've arrived and everything? She'll be missing you."

"She's not written to me. She said she'd write. She said there'd be a letter waiting for me when we got here."

Mrs Blakeman had noticed. Nobody had written, not even Prill's best friend Angela who always sent letters when they were separated. There had been no letters at all.

"I'm sorry about what happened, Auntie Jeannie." A tear ran slowly down Oliver's left cheek.

"Don't worry about that now, no harm was done. Off you go to bed." She hugged him but he went off looking utterly miserable. Prill felt sorry for him.

"So much for the wonderful engineer," Mum said gloomily, putting Alison on the bed to change her. Prill went away. She didn't know exactly how phones worked but she felt secretly that if a man came a thousand times to mend this one it would make no difference. The fact that it didn't work was nothing to do with cables or electrical impulses.

Something was closing in on them and driving them

slowly but relentlessly into a dark place, where there was loneliness and some kind of immense suffering. Wherever that place was, phones did not ring, letters were not delivered, pain and sickness came inexplicably and were not relieved. Over everything was the stink and rottenness of death itself.

And all of them had been touched by it in some way. Except Oliver. Why was he on the outside of everything? He was only unhappy now because of what had nearly happened to Donal Morrissey. The house itself held no terrors for him. In a little while he would probably drift off to sleep quite peacefully.

She and Colin hadn't really been fair to him. If they'd been a bit more friendly from the beginning he might not have gone off on his own, then the fire wouldn't have happened. She decided to talk to him tomorrow. Oliver was clever. He was so clear-thinking and cool, wise beyond his years. Talking to him might actually be a relief.

In Dr Moynihan's dream kitchen there was an electric deep-fryer the size of a small aquarium. Mum switched it on.

"Right. Chips, beans and sausages," she announced firmly. "Come on, we're all hungry. Don't mope around, Prill, let's just be grateful Alison's nodded off. You can speak to Dad tomorrow morning."

Prill didn't reply. Her mother's forced cheerfulness grated on her; she hated people jollying her along when she felt really miserable. She decided to feed the dog. When the human race got too much to bear there was always Jessie, faithful, loving, a bit mad.

But even she was in a mood. At the first sniff of dinner she was usually there at your feet, wagging her tail and butting her head into your legs till you gave her the dish. But now, when Prill put her meal down on the glossy kitchen tiles, she hardly looked at it, and when the girl stroked her neck and made a few coaxing noises, she shook her off irritably and gave a low growl, slinking off to her lair under the table where nobody would bother with her.

"I'll peel the spuds," Colin said, wanting to hurry the meal up. He had griping pains in his stomach again. He felt like eating a horse. Silently Prill got cups and plates out and banged them miserably on the kitchen table. "D'you know where the vegetables are, Mum?" he asked.

"In the utility room, on that tiled counter. I thought it would be the coolest place to store them." She was trying to use the electric tin opener. "Never seen one of these before. Wonder how it works?"

Colin was soon back with a polythene bag. His mother looked across at him. "What on earth's the matter? You've gone really pale."

"Are these the ones?"

"Yes. Don't you remember? We stopped and bought them on the way out of Dublin."

Prill had gone to get ready for bed. He shut the door into the hall so she wouldn't hear him. "Look," he said.

The bag had held ten pounds of potatoes. All that remained of them was a blackish slime. It looked as if they had somehow burst open; now they were just empty skins covered with a dark, spongy substance that had oozed out into the bag and was turning rapidly into a greeny-brown fungus. The bad smell was indescribable, and a black liquid was dripping from the corners of the bag, making inky stains on the kitchen floor.

"I just don't believe it. I bought *ten pounds* of them. Ugh, close the bag for goodness' sake and throw them away. It must be this weather, though I chose the coolest place I could think of."

Colin went outside to the dustbins. He threw the bag in and covered it with several layers of newspaper. Then he rammed the lid on tight. Even then he could smell it, that stinking sweetness that made his stomach curdle and brought a foul taste into his mouth. The heat was nothing to do with it. The heat had nothing to do with the milk either, the milk that had turned to a grey jelly in the jug.

He still had stomach pains. In the kitchen his mother was standing in front of the fridge-freezer. "Look what I've found," she said triumphantly. "A bag of frozen chips. I'm sure Dr Moynihan won't mind if we use them."

"Mum, I really don't think I want any. I had an enormous piece of cake up at the farm. I'm… I'm not hungry any more."

"Neither am I," Prill said. She was sitting at the table in her dressing-gown, brushing her hair. From her bedroom window she'd watched Colin throwing the potatoes away.

"What's the matter with everyone?" Mrs Blakeman said. "Doesn't *anyone* want anything to eat?" Neither of them answered, then Prill said blankly, "Alison's crying again, by the way. That didn't last long."

The night was so broken up with noise and climbing in and out of bed, nobody could say whether they'd actually been to sleep or not. Only Oliver slumbered on blissfully through everything. Nothing seemed capable of rousing him, not even the storm that blew fitfully all night, rattling the windows and hurling bad-tempered squalls against the glass. Colin and Prill lay awake, listening to the thunder, hoping that the violent showers would bring the temperature down. But it felt hotter than ever, and Colin was sweating inside the sleeping bag.

He could smell that mustiness in the room again. At one point he shone his torch on the ceiling. The faint grey lines he'd noticed yesterday were thickening gradually and the corners of the room were blurry, as if festooned with cobwebs. Oliver had said it couldn't possibly be mould, either he'd dreamed it or it was dampness coming out of the plaster. The builders should have waited much longer, he said, before decorating. He was such a know-all.

Prill heard her mother get up with Alison and traced her steps to the kitchen, bathroom, then back to bed. It happened half a dozen times and the baby never seemed to stop crying. Poor Mum. No wonder she was irritable.

Why was everything so much worse at night? Prill could bear the day, if they could get right away from the bungalow, swim, take Jessie for long walks, or just lie in the sun on that peaceful headland. But now, in the small hours, there was no

Chapter Eight

escape. As she lay in bed a fearful darkness seemed to press down upon her, like a great hand, and her mind would not let her sleep.

Three or four times she found herself standing by the window, so hot she could hardly breathe, staring out at the sweep of green field with the gate in one corner.

And the woman came again, quickly this time, as if she'd seen Prill. The girl saw her move rapidly down towards the house, stumbling as she ran and falling forward into the slime of the field, her dark cloak plastered to her by the streaming rain.

As before there was a blankness in which Prill saw nothing, then the face, with its silent, agonized scream, was thrust up against the window, the leaf hands plucking at the catch, and suddenly she felt cold air, and the sound of a window being pushed open.

She fled from the room in absolute terror, a hard lump blocking the scream that was forcing itself into her throat. She turned round to see if the woman was behind her, but blackness smothered everything and she was crashing into walls and furniture as she thrashed about in the darkness, trying to find the door.

The cold gust had come from the hall window. It was wide open and Colin stood in front of it, staring out into the night. Prill clutched at his hand. It felt clammy and cold and he was trembling.

"What's up?" she whispered. "Have you still got stomach ache?"

For a minute he didn't answer but went on looking at the rain. Then he closed the window firmly and stared at her.

"You look awful. What on earth's the matter?"

"Nothing… *nothing*," she said. It was only a dream. If she pretended it hadn't happened it might go away, like toothache the minute you've decided to go to the dentist. She felt better with Colin. It was better not to talk about it. If she denied her very existence the woman might not come again. She said, "Oh, I was dreaming, that's all. It was mixed up with the thunder, and Alison kept waking me when she cried. It's just hopeless trying to get a good night's sleep in this place." Then she looked at Colin. His face was putty-coloured. "Did you dream, too?"

He shook his head and said slowly, "No, I don't think I was dreaming, I'd not even gone to sleep. I saw somebody, just outside the window, somebody looking in. I'm positive." He stared out at the darkness, as if just looking might bring the person back.

"But it's three in the morning, and look how wild it is. Who'd be creeping round out there at this time?" He looked so frightened Prill tried to put the question in a calm, reasoning voice. But she didn't fool him, or herself.

"There *was* someone, Prill, and I wasn't asleep."

"Who was it?"

"I couldn't see the face till they came right up to the window, but it looked a bit like Donal Morrissey. He had a red thing over his head."

"But he's at Father Hagan's. The O'Malleys said so. He's

Chapter Eight

staying there till they've mended his van."

"Well, perhaps he's come back. I'm sure that's who it was. I did see someone, I'd swear on the Bible."

They had both had the same dream. If it was a dream. The Morrissey face peering in at them through the driving rain, that withered, pain-filled face that accused and begged them, silently.

"I saw it too," formed on Prill's lips, but she swallowed the words back. Instead she went down the passage towards the kitchen.

"What are you going to do?"

"Make myself a drink, look up Dr Moynihan's phone number, then go back to bed."

"And then what?"

"I'm not waiting for them to come back to the phone. There'll be a phone box in Ballimagliesh. I'll go there and get through to Dad on my own."

"I think everything would be OK if he came back," Colin said thoughtfully. "Mum's not herself, is she? She's being horrible to Alison. What's got into her?"

"It's not just Mum, or Alison. You know that as well as I do. I just think we should pack up and leave. I'm going to tell Dad that."

"Don't you think that's going a bit far?" Colin said, but in a voice that lacked all conviction. "I shouldn't think he'll want to give up the portrait. Anyway, couldn't it just be the weather, and this bug we've got, and everything? I think we've started imagining things."

"I think it's this house. I know it's very modern and expensive but there's something terribly wrong with it. I know there is."

"What do you think's happening to us?"

"I don't know. But it's threatening us, it's trying to hurt us. Colin, I think we're in danger. We should go home."

Chapter Nine

KEVIN O'MALLEY CAME down at eight the next morning with a can of milk and brought a message from his mother. "Dr O'Keefe is away on holiday, missus, but they've told her Dr Donovan will call on you."

"When will that be, Kevin? Did they give your mother any idea?"

He looked doubtful. "Not really. Dr Donovan's a bit slow getting round to people these days, he's retired really. But they did say he'd come. It'll be afternoon I'm thinking, so if you're going out—"

"I think I'd better make a phone call myself. Ours is off again. Do you think your mother—"

"Sorry, missus, but our phone isn't working either. It was last night's gale. The lines are down all along the Ballimagliesh road."

Irrationally Colin felt rather relieved. The O'Malleys' phone was broken, too, so it wasn't just the bungalow. He knew quite well theirs had gone dead hours before the storm blew up but he refused to think about that. There was strange comfort in the fact that they were all cut off.

Kevin was looking at Alison. "The baby looks grand," he said cheerfully. But he did notice how thin she was. His mam had kicked herself yesterday for mentioning it, but she was right.

"Ye-es," Mrs Blakeman said slowly. "She's as right as rain this morning, though she gave us a terrible night. She's such a moody little thing. One minute she's all smiles, next minute she's screaming the place down. That's why it's so difficult, knowing whether to bother a doctor."

"I would, Auntie Jeannie," Oliver said suddenly. "Babies don't cry for nothing. I don't think she's well. My mother says you should never take risks, especially with children and old people."

Everyone was surprised. He'd said nothing at breakfast, apart from things like "Pass the sugar". They all thought he was sulking, or still feeling embarrassed about yesterday. But he spoke with such conviction, as if he'd been thinking about it all privately and drawing his own secret conclusions. What else had he heard, noticed, decided upon? Prill was going to talk to him the minute her mother's back was turned.

"Well, to be sure the doctor will call," Kevin repeated, looking up at the sky. It was warmer than ever, but there was no sun, and thunder was still grumbling somewhere in the distance. "There's another storm forecast," he said. "A real beauty. If you do go out, I wouldn't go far."

Colin and Prill spent the whole morning helping Oliver. He'd dug quite a bit of soil out already. He was obviously stronger than he looked, in spite of his illness.

"When did you do all this, Oll?" Prill said. "*Ouch!*" She pulled at a great chunk of stone and scraped the skin off her fingers in the process.

"This morning. I was up very early and that Kevin O'Malley helped me a bit yesterday. He's strong, he is. Said he'd bring me a piece of tin for the roof. Don't suppose he'll bother now, though." He went on digging fiercely. All this embarrassment, regret and hurt over Donal Morrissey's van were expressed in his furious scrabbling and poking at the hard-packed earth. It showered behind him and settled in everyone's hair and clothes. Within half an hour they were all filthy. It was a good thing prim Auntie Phyllis wasn't there to see Oliver.

At first Colin felt stupid, digging a hideout for his small cousin. He'd grown out of all that. But slowly the idea took hold of him and he actually started to enjoy it. There was something very satisfactory about thrusting the spade into a bank of solid earth, twisting the blade round to work it loose, then removing it in shovelfuls. He decided to get as dirty as possible, then, when he was too hot to bear it any longer, run down to the beach for a swim. The tide would be just right in a couple of hours.

Prill's contribution was more artistic. She was working her way round the walls with a garden trowel, smoothing them over carefully and pulling out all the stones. Oliver worked beside her, stopping now and then to examine his spadeful of earth.

"Found anything interesting?" she asked him.

"Only what I showed you and some more bits of china. Oh, and the remains of a dog," he added casually.

"A *dog*?"

"Yes. Well, I think that's what it was. My father dug one up in our garden once, it looked the same. There were just a few bones. I put them in a bag, under that hedge."

"Ugh. Do they smell?"

"No, not really. D'you want to see them?"

"No *thanks*."

Colin came over and looked at their end of the hole. The "den" now measured two metres in length and Oliver was widening his bit.

"It's not very deep yet, is it? How far down d'you intend going, Oll?"

"Well, I'd like to stand up in it, when the roof's on."

"It'll mean a lot more digging then."

Privately Colin thought he was crackers. They'd abandon the project long before that point was reached. And yet Oliver was so determined, he was working away like a giant mole, as if his life depended on it. Colin wanted to laugh but part of him was impressed by the small boy's determination. Prill was right. There was something very odd about Oliver.

Chapter Nine

After about an hour Colin chucked his spade down. "I'm boiling. I'm going in for a drink."

"Bring us one," Prill shouted. She had just found her first bit of pottery and Oliver was cleaning it expertly with his toothbrush. Soon Colin was back with some biscuits and a bottle of fizzy lemonade. They all sat dangling their legs over the edge of the hole, swigging from the bottle in turn.

"Where's Mum?"

"In the kitchen, walking Alison to sleep. She says she's not going out till the doctor's been."

Prill could just see her mother pacing the kitchen floor with the baby flopped over one shoulder. She was trying to croon her to sleep, and reading a book at the same time. Quite suddenly she said to Oliver, "We think there's something wrong with this house, Oll." It came out in a loud, impassioned burst. Her cousin went on drinking lemonade and didn't even look at her.

Then he said, "Yes, I think there might be. You never know, perhaps it's haunted."

His flat, matter-of-fact voice struck a chill into her. "So you *knew* something was wrong and you didn't even tell us?"

"Well, you didn't ask me. Nobody's bothered with me since we arrived."

Prill felt uncomfortable and there was a stiff silence. Then Colin said, "Why d'you say 'haunted', Oliver? How can people be haunted by a smell, and things going mouldy?"

He shrugged. "I don't know. It's very complicated. But I can tell you one thing, Mr Catchpole's aunt in Dorset was haunted once, by an old woman, and before she saw her there was always this smell of bacon frying."

"Who's Mr Catchpole?"

"An old man who lives in our house. He's a friend of mine."

"I wouldn't mind bacon," Prill said. "But this smell! Yuk, it's foul."

"I'm sure it's the smell that's making us feel sick all the time and giving me these stomach pains," Colin added. "Perhaps that's what's wrong with Alison."

"Perhaps," Oliver repeated, kicking at the side of the hole. Then he said, "But you've not actually seen anything, have you?"

"No," Prill admitted. "But we've had some awful nightmares, and last night we both had the same dream. I thought it was a woman, but Colin thinks it was Donal Morrissey."

Oliver jumped when he heard that name. He'd been thinking about nobody else all morning. Much earlier in the day, next to the dog's bones, he had come across something else. It was the greatest find he'd ever had. He'd cleaned it up, put it in a little box, and hidden it with the plastic sack under the hedge. When the right moment came, and the old man had calmed down again, he planned to take it up to the caravan.

"Well, I dreamed about him too," he said, trying to speak calmly, "but then my father says that you often dream about the last thing that happened just before you went to bed. I don't think that means anything."

Chapter Nine

"But why is it happening to *us*, Oliver? That's the frightening thing. This place doesn't seem to have the same effect on you. You don't feel sick or anything, do you? Nobody's had a proper night's sleep since we got here, except you."

"I know. I've been thinking about that. Perhaps it's something to do with your family, something I'm not part of."

"But you *are* family, you're our cousin."

"I'm adopted."

"Well, you don't think we're imagining everything, do you, Oliver?" Prill said, suddenly feeling quite desperate. "That's what Colin keeps saying." She was trying hard not to cry. Actually spelling her fears out was making it worse somehow, not better.

"No, I shouldn't think so," he answered in a flat, uninterested voice, climbing back into his hole. "It's what my father's always saying."

"And what's that?" Colin said coldly. He was really irritated by Oliver. He was behaving like a lump of dough, as if these terrifying things happened to lots of people every day. And he was fed up of hearing the sayings of Uncle Stanley and Auntie Phyllis.

Oliver took a deep breath and spouted, "There are more things in heaven and earth, Horatio, than are dreamt of in your philosophy."

"And what's that supposed to mean when it's at home?" Colin said rudely.

"Well, he's always saying that. I think it's Shakespeare."

"But what does it *mean*?"

"Just that everything's happened to someone, at one time or another, and that nobody should laugh at ghost stories, I suppose."

"Nobody's laughing, Oliver," Colin said bitterly. He sounded so offhand, so indifferent, he deserved to be bashed over the head with a spade.

Chapter Ten

PRILL WALKED UP the track to the main road swinging a shopping bag and thinking about her cousin. It was a pity Colin had lost his temper; if Oliver hadn't rubbed him up the wrong way they might have got somewhere. She had noticed how he'd jumped when Donal Morrissey's name was mentioned. He seemed obsessed with the old man somehow.

There was hardly any food in the house. Prill had offered to walk the two miles to the shops in Ballimagliesh and she'd insisted on going alone. "No umbrella, thank you, and *no dog*," she'd said firmly. Jessie had perked up a bit and eaten a huge breakfast. Perhaps she and Alison had got the same kind of bug – all smiles one minute and total misery the next. Now she was desperate for a walk, but Prill left her with Oliver, Colin, and Kevin O'Malley who were all digging enthusiastically. The dog was back on form and driving them mad, jumping down into the hole and scrabbling for imaginary rabbits.

There was a V.G. supermarket in Ballimagliesh, but Mrs O'Malley had recommended Mooneys' Stores, at the far end of the village. They sold good bacon there, she said, and home-made bread.

It was a boring walk. On the right the sea was a snatch of muddy blue across the fields and scrubby farmland sloped up on the left, broken by clumps of trees and the occasional house. The road shot straight ahead as far as she could see and on the horizon, under two enormous elms, she spotted two small figures with hands thrust out. Surely they weren't trying to thumb a lift into the village? Some hope on a road like this. No one had driven past her since she'd started walking.

As she drew level they turned and looked at her. They were children, a boy of about fourteen and a younger girl, both swamped in what looked like tattered woolly ponchos with tasselled hoods. They must be terribly hot.

But their feet were bare. Prill hadn't worn shoes since they'd arrived, neither had Colin. It was only Oliver who'd insisted on putting socks and sneakers on every single morning but it hadn't seemed so hot to him. She only wore sandals now because of the metalled road. They were standing on the grass where it was cooler.

As she went past the boy plucked at her arm. "Please, could you spare something?" His voice was only a whisper and seemed to come from deep inside a creaking chest. In the quietness she could hear his breath rattling. The girl said nothing but she too thrust her hand out, a tiny withered hand, more like a claw.

Prill had a five-pound note for the shopping and some coins of her own wrapped in a scrap of paper with Dr Moynihan's Dublin phone number on it. She daren't part with those. She might need them all for the phone box, to speak to her father. "I'm sorry," she said, "I haven't got anything."

"*Please,*" the boy said again, and his fingers dug into her arm. A faint croak came from the girl; she was opening her mouth and shaping words but only a peculiar animal noise came out. As she leaned forwards to grab at Prill her face emerged from the brown hood. It was white and pinched, the skin semi-transparent like muslin cloth, covered all over with fine down. Both faces looked misshapen and shrunk, more like monkeys than children.

The fingernails were biting into her flesh. She was getting frightened and tried to pull her arm away. "Let me go, both of you, *please*. I've told you, I haven't *got* any money."

"*Please,*" the boy said again. The girl just opened and shut her mouth, like a fish. Prill screamed and gave a violent tug but the two children held on strongly. In the end she pushed at them ferociously and kicked hard at their bare legs. The small girl yelped like a puppy and fell back on the grass. Prill broke free and found herself running along the hard, yellow road with red spattering her T-shirt. The nails had made four bloody half-moons on her left arm.

Finally a stitch forced her to slow down but she still

walked rapidly. At last the first houses of Ballimagliesh appeared in a green dip below her. As she dropped down off the hill she glanced backwards fearfully. The children had disappeared. Seconds later a blue van rattled past with three people inside. "Reagan: Plumbing Contractors" was painted on the side. She hoped desperately she wouldn't see them again, but Ballimagliesh was only a tiny place.

A broad, brown field, already striped by the plough, swept down to the road behind the first cottages. As Prill walked past she saw somebody moving very slowly along the furrows, with a bundle in its arms. The shape was dark, almost lost against the brown-black of the soil, but there was something about the way it jerked and stumbled down towards the road that plunged her into nightmare.

"Pull yourself together and stop imagining things," she told herself angrily, and stood quite still for a minute, right in the middle of the village street. Then she put her hand against her forehead. She definitely felt feverish, her temperature must be over a hundred. It must be this fluey feeling that Colin had complained about. If they sold aspirins at Mooneys' Stores she'd better buy some.

The plumber's van was parked a few houses down and a man in overalls was lolling against it, chatting to an old woman in a doorway. There was no sign of the two children and the ploughed field was empty, so was the muddy lane that joined it to the pavement.

Prill spotted a telephone box at the far end of the street and began to walk towards it. Next door she found Mooneys'

Stores with dustbins and mops displayed outside. It was the kind of shop that sold everything. A comforting baking smell wafted through the door. She hesitated, then went inside.

The shop was gloomy and full of people waiting. Prill edged past them trying to make out what was on the shelves. Why was it so dark inside? There was hardly enough light to read her mother's shopping list. Then she remembered, there was a power cut in Ballimagliesh. They were doing some maintenance work, Mrs O'Malley had told her. That would be why they'd rigged up this smelly oil-lamp that smoked and spluttered over her head.

When a wave of fresh customers came in Prill was pushed to one side. People jostled each other and tried to get to the front of the queue. But it was strangely quiet. All she could hear was money chinking and things being slid across the counter. The shop was so crowded she couldn't raise her arm to hold the list under the lamp. When her turn came she'd give it to the shopkeeper, that would be the quickest. She wanted to get out really, she could hardly breathe in this stuffy place.

The shop door rattled again and Prill glanced back. Her heart warmed to see the fat face of a clergyman. It just had to be that Father Hagan. Oliver was right, he was a bit like Friar Tuck. She smiled at him. But he had already turned his back to talk to someone. She just caught the words "tobacco", "very difficult" and "old Donal". Then she heard something else. An argument was going on at the counter. The general mumbling in the queue died away and everyone leaned forward to listen.

But the customer clearly didn't want anybody to hear. Prill could only make out the tone of the voice, the note of pleading. Then she heard, "Give me what you have then," from the shopkeeper. "We've got little enough ourselves, God knows." And suddenly, very close, she could see a hand thrust out at him, with the fingers drawn tightly over the palm, shrivelled yellowing fingers like turkey claws.

It lay lifeless on the bare counter and Prill watched the plump, pink hand of the man prise the fingers open slowly, one by one, revealing nothing.

"I'm sorry, but if you have no money at all…" Then the words turned into mumbling again. The woman's voice deadened into a low, monotonous keening. It was the most desolate sound Prill had ever heard.

Suddenly there was a shriek. "For the love of God, spare me *something*!" Then several things happened at once. The shop door blew shut with a bang and buckets rolled over the floor. Prill heard Father Hagan wheezing at the back, helping another man stack them up again and laughing. A strip light over the counter was flickering into life and the tubby, white-overalled shopkeeper blinked up at it. In that instant the shawled figure at the counter leaned forward and grabbed.

A neat pyramid of loaves, buns and cakes toppled over. "Take what I have, and may God help me," the woman cried shrilly and, pulling a bundle from under her arm, she thrust it at the goggling shop owner.

Chapter Ten

As she pushed past, Prill could smell the new loaf in her hand. The swinging oil-lamp turned the woman's face a muddy yellow and patched the shrunken face with shadow. The girl saw the familiar domed head, the remains of springy, russet hair, the gaunt cheekbones almost breaking the flesh.

All the lights were back on in the shop and the man was reading her list and saying pleasantly, "I'll get you a little box for this surely. Oh, you've got a bag? If you'll give it to me then. The bacon's out at the back, I won't be a minute."

As she waited, Prill fingered the sacking bundle lightly, then laid her whole hand flat upon it. A coldness came up through the coarse webbing. She pushed at it. The lump inside was heavy, unyielding, and gave off a high, gamey smell.

Her fingers crept to the end of the sacking where the loose brown folds had fallen open. She could hear the bacon-slicer whining faintly in the back room, and Father Hagan chatting away somewhere behind her. She didn't want to unwrap the bundle, she wanted to run out of the shop. But something compelled her to roll the thing over and over on the counter till the sacking fell away, and with it the layer of filthy rags underneath. Then she could see properly.

The smell coming out of the bundle was like very bad meat. But what Prill saw, lying on the counter, was a human child. The tiny body was naked, the face blotched and swollen, the eyes glazed in a white, expressionless stare like a fish on a slab. It looked like Alison.

She remembered the shopkeeper coming back with the

bacon and staring at her open-mouthed as she stood clutching the countertop, staring down at the dead baby, screaming the one word "No!" over and over again. She remembered him scuttling into the back shouting for his wife, "Maraid! Maraid! Come here, for God's sake!" Then a sick darkness wrapped itself round her as she plunged about on the shop floor, knocking into displays of pans and glasses when she crashed to the ground.

She remembered getting outside and being sick against a mossy, white-washed wall, and Father Hagan peering down at her anxiously as the blood from a cut on her head streamed down her face, like warm rain.

Chapter Eleven

"WELL, YOU WERE wrong about the weather," Colin said, climbing out of the hole. "It's hotter than ever, I think. Oh, get off, Jessie!"

"Mmm," Kevin mumbled, looking up at the sky. "But there's a lot of rain up there. It's got to come down sooner or later. Anyway, I'm going now. I've got to help my dad."

Colin felt disappointed. He really liked Kevin O'Malley, and he was a much better companion than his cousin. Oliver was so slow, so pernickety, always stopping to inspect what he'd dug up and shouting bossily, "Hey! Don't touch that! We're not up to there yet." He could be so babyish. Kevin had just grinned to himself and humoured him. After all, it was his hole.

"Do you want to come with us? We've got some land on the high ground, the other side of Ballimagliesh. We're cutting peat for the winter. You can give us a hand if you like."

Colin didn't need to think twice. "OK. I'll just check with my mother. Should I bring this?"

"No. We've got special spades for that job. Do you want to come, Oliver?" Kevin called down the hole.

"Oh, *no*," Colin was thinking. But Oliver didn't even look up.

"No, thank you," he said politely. "I've got some more work to do on this."

"It's surely deep enough now?" Kevin said. "When I bring you the sacking, and that piece of corrugated iron, it'll be a grand little den."

"Oh, let him get on with it," Colin whispered, impatient to get away. "The rate he digs there's not much danger of him shaking anybody's foundations. We did most of the work this morning. Are you ready? I can come. My mother's waiting in for the doctor."

Kevin shrugged. "All right. Goodbye now, Oliver." He was thinking that the Blakeman boy hadn't got much patience with his small cousin. He'd liked dens himself when he was little, especially when his father let him play in the bales and make one there after harvest. But he'd never actually dug himself a hole. It was a great idea that was, it took brains.

Oliver may well be fussing over his hole like an old woman, but if you approached everything at top speed, like Colin, like a bull at a gate, you could miss a lot. You had to stop now and then, to work out what you'd done so far. That's what his father always said.

Chapter Eleven

Take a den for example. Colin obviously hadn't noticed something that Oliver thought was very important, something he'd only spotted in the last half hour. You could only see it properly if you looked into the hole from above, at a certain angle.

Right in the middle, where he'd just been digging, someone must have dug once before. The soil was different, crumblier and lighter in colour, and there was a definite shape to it. It was a rough oval, about a metre across.

It was a hole within a hole and it was directly above this that Oliver had unearthed the dog. Now he was uncovering handfuls of moist, peaty stuff, like black matting, with the shapes of twigs and leaves still visible in it.

He'd put everything of importance in a black plastic rubbish sack under some bushes. The bones were in it, and the bits of pottery and the clay pipe. Only the treasures for Donal Morrissey were ready in their box, transferred to the pocket of his trousers.

Auntie Jeannie was sitting at the kitchen table reading, with her back to the window. The baby was asleep presumably. He didn't intend to disturb her, in case there were awkward questions. He scribbled, "Gone for a short walk," on a scrap of paper and weighted it down with a stone. Jessie opened one eye as Oliver crept about. She was tied up again. It was the first time she'd not barked at him and she looked strangely listless. It must be the heat, he decided. Then he smiled at himself. He was saying it now. It was the Blakeman explanation for everything.

But it was hot. He peeled off his sweater, left it neatly folded by the note, then started to walk rapidly along the track.

The door of the caravan was propped open with an old broom and he saw an upturned yellow bucket next to it, crowned with a scrubbing brush. A pile of neatly cut new timbers lay close by, together with a collection of tools. The O'Malleys must think a lot of Donal Morrissey. They'd already started repairing the van and someone had been inside, washing the floor. The old man wouldn't like that much; old people got agitated if you moved their things.

There was nobody about but Oliver still looked round carefully before climbing up into the van. The vegetable patch was now a pathetic black square. The scorched remains of stalks and leaves lay twisted together on the ashy ground, and last night's rain had turned everything tarry. His rubber soles made black, striped marks on the clean floor.

The van was lighter inside and smelt much fresher. The tiny windows had been rubbed clean and the smelly dog blanket had disappeared. It was probably tumbling round in Mrs O'Malley's washing machine by now. Donal wouldn't like that either.

He sat down on an old stool, took the little box from his pocket and put it in front of him on the table. Then he looked round. Mrs O'Malley certainly hadn't cleaned the shelves, the piles of tins and boxes were so thickly furred with dust nobody could have touched them in years. But one of them was quite shiny; it was on its own in a corner, next to a cracked mug and some old pipes. It looked as if someone had polished it.

Oliver went over and lifted it up. It was quite heavy and rattled. Very carefully he put it on the table and sat down again.

His fingers itched. This would be the old man's treasure box, where he kept all his precious, most private things. Mr Catchpole had one too, but it wasn't as big as this. There was a brass lock, but when Oliver lifted the lid it gave way. He pushed it right back and looked inside. Whatever the box contained was hidden by folds of thick yellow newspaper. Oliver's little finger played with one corner of it. He couldn't stop now.

Then a dog barked outside. Oliver pushed the box right away from him and stood up, but Donal Morrissey had swung himself up into the van before he could get through the door. The dog snarled, straining at the end of a short rope, and the old man stared at him in disbelief across the rickety table.

Oliver, trembling and white-faced, was starting to sweat in the strange heat. Donal Morrissey's eyes were bloodshot and bulging, weariness filled his crumpled, bony face. So the boy had come a second time, and he'd just walked all the way back from Father Hagan's place in Ballimagliesh, to be on his own again, to have some peace.

Oh, he didn't blame him for starting the fire, not now the Father had explained it all to him. Donal thought the lad may well be a bit weak in the head. He'd been very ill apparently, perhaps it had affected him. There was a funny look in his eyes, and he was plainly terrified, twisting his fingers about, his thin shoulders shaking. Donal Morrissey pitied him. He wasn't such an ogre. He'd seen a lot of things in his time, lived through most things.

But even though he looked frightened, the boy sat down again and began to speak. His voice was loud and penetrating. He knew exactly what he wanted to say, he'd been rehearsing it all morning while he was digging.

"Mr Morrissey," he burst out, "I came to say that I'm very sorry about your van. It was a mistake. I was just trying to help you, that's all, so you wouldn't be without something to eat in the winter."

The old man went on staring at him. Then he noticed his box on the table. Eileen O'Malley must have polished it. She was welcome, she knew that box well. She'd sat on his knee many a time, in the old days, and played with some of the things inside.

"Go home," he said suddenly. "I know what you did. It doesn't matter any more, boy. Go home, I'm telling you." After the long walk his legs were starting to buckle underneath him. He was getting much weaker. He sat down abruptly, opposite Oliver.

The boy's mouth quivered. He put his little box into the old man's hand. Donal's words had been gentle enough but his voice was harsh, like rooks cawing. Oliver hated it. The man didn't really believe he was sorry, and he was.

Chapter Eleven

All Donal Morrissey wanted at that moment was to be on his own with his old dog, to make his fire up, brew a mug of tea, and sit quietly in his own caravan. Now this strange boy had arrived, wanting to give him something.

"This is for you. I often dig things up, and it's the best thing I've ever found." Wearily the old man reached out, took the box, opened it, and shook the contents into his hand. In his cracked palm lay a small, round, metal object, about the size of a walnut, stuck on to a bit of rotten wood. It rattled when he shook it.

"I tried to clean a bit of it. I think it might be silver. There's an initial on it, look, where I've rubbed."

The old man's eyes were watering but he didn't need to look at the initial, he'd seen something very like it many times before. On the flat side of the metal walnut someone had engraved a curly capital "M".

"And I found this with it." Oliver took an old envelope from his pocket and removed something from it very carefully, with a finger and thumb, a scrap of purply-red material about five centimetres square. "There was quite a lot of this, but it all crumbled away when I touched it. There were some bits of wood too. Perhaps everything had been in a box."

The old man looked at the silver nut and the scrap of glowing silk for a long time, then he placed them on the lid of his treasure box with a shaking hand.

"Where did you find these things?"

"Where we've been digging. I'm making a den. It's just

outside the back door, at the bungalow."

"Was anyone else there?"

"No. My two cousins came to help later but I didn't show them. They think I'm stupid. Well, Colin does."

Oliver looked up into Donal Morrissey's face. To his astonishment he saw that the old man's eyes had tears in them. "You are not stupid," he said. "And I like what you've brought me, I like it very much. But go home now, they'll be missing you at the house, and I want to go to sleep."

As Oliver went through the door he clutched at him quite fiercely. "Promise me something, will you, boy? If you should find anything else like this *bring it to me*."

"Can I tell anybody?" Oliver didn't think he'd want to tell, not for a minute, but it was as well to know what was allowed. There should always be rules about secrets like this, in his opinion.

"Nobody at all, I'm thinking," the old man said firmly. "Unless it's the priest. I'll be showing Father Hagan this. You can tell him, surely."

Every night, when he got back from Danny's Bar, Donal Morrissey set the contents of his box out on the filthy table. Today he didn't wait for darkness. Before Oliver was halfway home he had lifted off the newspapers and taken out three things: a shabby black prayer book, a tattered square of dark red silk, and a baby's rattle. The handle was apple-wood carved with tiny leaves, the top a hollow silver oval with a wavy initial carved on one side. He arranged them in front of him, next to Oliver's present, then looked carefully from one to the other. Every time the box came out he gave that rattle a bit of a polish, and it was most nights now. Nobody came to see him these days, except the priest and John O'Malley.

He shook the rattle and the noise made the dog bark suddenly. "Husht, will you," and he nudged it gently with his foot. Then he unfolded his piece of silk and looked at the light through it, marvelling at the way the patterns bloodied the sky into flowing purples and strange reds.

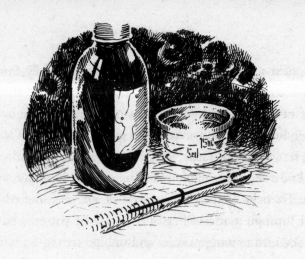

Chapter Twelve

PRILL WOKE UP and found herself under a blanket on a hard sofa, next to a smoky fire. She'd come round once before when someone had dabbed her forehead with cold water and applied sticking plasters. Then she'd passed out again.

Father Hagan sat opposite in a fat, over-stuffed chair, sucking on a pipe and looking straight at her. It was dark in the little room. Through the window she could see a neat cabbage patch and a square of thick yellow sky.

"Is this your house?"

"It is. You fainted in the shop, then you were sick. Do you remember? Lucky I was around. This house is just two doors past Mooneys' Stores. So how are you feeling now, dear?"

"All right."

It wasn't true. She was feeling bilious and unbearably hot again. Where was her shopping bag and the precious bit of

Chapter Twelve

paper? She still hadn't phoned her father.

"We went for Dr Donovan, but he's out on his rounds. Anyway, they tell me he's calling on your mother later this afternoon to look at the baby. So he'll see you too. Is the little one not very well then?"

Prill found his gentle kindness quite unbearable, after all that had happened. "No," she whispered. "No, she isn't at all well," and she started to cry.

Something in the man's face told her he would listen and try to understand. It was the same thing Dad had seen and wanted to paint. It was nothing to do with his being a priest, or with the simple crucifix hanging on the wall. She couldn't say what it was exactly, she just knew he wouldn't say her story was stupid, or all made up.

Once the tears started she couldn't stop them. Father Hagan heard everything from the beginning, how she'd disliked the bungalow the minute she'd set foot in it and how she hadn't wanted Dad to leave them there. She told him about the strange smell on the beach, and about the mustiness in Colin's room, and about her nightmares, that figure crawling across the blackened fields towards the house, and the wasted face looking in at her, the fact that Colin had seen the same face.

Father Hagan sat up when she said this. So far he thought he could give explanations for everything she'd told him, but this was different. If the girl was feverish, with a high temperature, she could have imagined all kinds of things. But she was insisting that the brother had shared her dream. That was more difficult to explain away.

Now she was telling him about the beggars on the road to Ballimagliesh. "I did see them," she sobbed. "They asked me for money. The boy stuck his nails into my arm and it bled. Look, if you don't believe me." She pulled the blanket back to show him. All he could see was a slim, sunburnt arm, slightly freckled. Without thinking, he shook his head.

This maddened Prill and she started to shout. She didn't know whether she was crying or screaming. "It's *true*. I don't care what my arm looks like now. I *did see them*, and I saw the baby!"

"Yes, well now, let's talk about that, dear. In the shop, was it? Try to keep calm, Prill. It's important to remember as much as you can. It will help you to talk about it." She had certainly been very violent in Mooneys' Stores. It wasn't exactly a fainting fit. He had been waiting at the back of the queue and seen everything. It seemed to him that the girl had had some kind of hysterical attack. She had kept poking crazily at something a delivery man had left on the counter, a ham he thought it was. Now she was telling him it was a child, a corpse, left there by a poor woman in exchange for a loaf of bread. All he had seen was the girl herself, plunging about the floor in a wreckage of paint cans and broken glass.

She raved on and on about the woman in the dream, and in the shop, but Father Hagan wasn't really listening now, he was studying her face. She definitely looked ill. The sooner he got her back to her mother, so Michael Donovan could take a look at her, the better for everyone. Poor child.

Chapter Twelve

He rarely used his ancient car. It was a temperamental beast and he could do most of his journeys on a bicycle. But today it started first time. "Ah," he said, with simple joy, "the grace of God." He helped Prill to climb in. She was shivering now so he got a rug and tucked it round her. He planned to drive very slowly so they could talk.

He said nothing till they were up the hill and out of Ballimagliesh, then he said tentatively, "Prill, dear, is this your first visit to Ireland?"

She nodded.

"Do you know anything about it, I'm wondering? Sure it's a land rich in history, every stick and stone of it."

"Not much," she said. "Oliver does, though. He knew all about the potato famine. His father teaches history, he made him read books about it before we came."

"Ah, yes. What about you, though? I'm just thinking, perhaps you've read something for yourself, have you, or watched a television programme? Might there be something you've seen that's worried you – you know, stuck in your mind? That's where our bad dreams come from, very often."

"No, I don't think so. Well, not that I can remember."

Father Hagan decided to shift his ground slightly. "Tell me about your cousin Oliver."

"I don't know very much. We don't see him often. He's only our second cousin, his mother's Mum's auntie. He's adopted."

"And does he know who his parents were?"

"No, I don't think so. I don't know that anyone does.

Auntie Phyllis – that's his mother – married Uncle Stanley when she was quite old, and after a while they fostered Oliver. They've adopted him now, I think."

Prill was hesitating. She didn't think Father Hagan would approve of her private jokes with Colin, about Oliver being found by the swings in Battersea Park, or left on some hospital steps in a Sainsbury's carton. But there *was* a mystery about him. She knew that because it was never discussed at home.

"Why are you so interested in Oliver?" she said sharply.

"Oh, nothing really… He's an unusual little boy though, isn't he, digging his hole and trying to save the old man's potatoes? An individual, I'd say." Father Hagan knew it sounded feeble. He couldn't tell Prill what he felt about Oliver, or how disturbed he'd been at their first meeting. He didn't understand it himself.

It was five o'clock when the car bumped its way down the track and parked outside the bungalow, next to Oliver's den. Mrs Blakeman was standing by the window looking out for them. Their phone was still dead but the farm was back on again, and Mrs O'Malley had been down to tell her Prill had fainted in Mooneys' Stores and that Father Hagan was bringing her home.

They had only been in the house ten minutes when a second car drew up outside and doors slammed. Then the bell was rung three times in quick succession. Mum tripped over the dog as she ran to answer it. Whoever it was had no time to waste.

Chapter Twelve

Dr Donovan didn't wait to be asked inside. Father Hagan was in the hall, on his way out. The man just shoved past him rudely, muttering, "Now then, where *is* this child? Humph, don't need to ask, do I? Just follow the screams. All right, all right, let's have a look at you. Come on, it's not the end of the world."

"Send one of the boys along if you need me," the priest whispered as he went through the front door. "I'll not get in the doctor's way. Don't want him to think I'm interfering or anything."

When the bell rang, Colin, Oliver and Alison had been eating tea at the kitchen table. They all looked up when the elderly doctor appeared in the doorway, and all three disliked him on sight. So did Mrs Blakeman, so did Prill, and when he touched her, Alison set up a wailing loud enough to wake the dead.

Under the table Jessie gave a sudden howl in sympathy. She seemed off colour again. Colin had persuaded her to eat her dinner but she'd been violently sick afterwards. It had upset them all. Everyone was fond of Jessie. Even Oliver had seemed concerned and offered advice. If Dr Donovan had been a bit kinder to Alison they might have asked him what was wrong. But the man was hopeless.

They could all smell the drink on his breath. Colin watched him fumble with the catches on his case, wondering whether the way he lurched and staggered across the kitchen floor was the result of too many whiskies or just extreme old age. He looked nearer eighty than seventy and was almost as decrepit as Donal Morrissey.

The baby screamed at the thermometer and screamed at the stethoscope. She went on screaming as the strange-smelling, whiskery old man inflicted his various cold instruments of torture upon her one by one.

Mrs Blakeman had been waiting for this visit all day. She'd had plenty of time to prepare what she wanted to say, but one look at Dr Donovan and the words died on her lips. She doubted that he would listen to her, even when sober. He'd hardly looked at Alison and he was already putting his instruments away. There was no point in asking him to examine Prill. All he wanted was to get home.

The truth was that the old man was well past making house calls on a sticky August day. He'd been dragged out of retirement because Dr O'Keefe was on holiday and the usual locum was ill. He'd had a long afternoon of difficult old women with imaginary aches and pains, neurotic mothers and snotty-nosed children.

This baby's temperature was normal, so was its pulse. It wasn't refusing its food and its bowels were in order. Nothing wrong with this child that a bit of firm handling wouldn't put right. The mother clearly spoiled it and was determined to worry. It was certainly on the thin side but that was all to the good. Fat babies were unhealthy.

He dumped two bottles of medicine on the kitchen table. "The pink – give her a couple of spoonfuls at bedtime if she's playing up. The white – that's for stomach upsets…warm weather…you never know, may just be hatching a little bug.

Come up to the surgery in a couple of days, if you're still not happy about her." Dr Donovan's pinched, lopsided face had a glassy look. It plainly said, "Don't you dare". Then he added, "She'll be as right as rain tomorrow."

In less than two minutes he was weaving his way up the track. Helplessly, Mrs Blakeman watched him go. "That's that then," she said blankly, going back into the kitchen and flopping down at the table. "He wasn't much help, was he? Mrs O'Malley did warn me."

"Wonder how many drinks he'd had?" Colin said darkly. Alison was still grizzling but more quietly now, more as a matter of routine. She was as pleased to see the back of Dr Donovan as everybody else.

Prill looked at the pink bottle, unscrewed the cap, and sniffed. "I know what this is. It's only baby aspirin in a kind of syrup. This is no good."

"I know, I know," her mother said wearily. "It's just happy juice. You both had it as babies. All it did was knock you out for a bit, so Dad and I could get some sleep. It doesn't really cure anything."

"What are we going to do, Mum?" Colin asked. "And what about Jessie? You said you'd ask him about her."

"I know," Mrs Blakeman said wearily. "But how *could* I? Oh, I just don't know. Perhaps Mr O'Malley's got something we could dose her with, but I don't like to keep running up there. I must speak to your father tomorrow. Somebody's got to have a phone that works. Surely the whole of Ireland can't be cut off? Anyway, I think I'll have a bath. Can you cope with Alison, between you? I don't think I can stand much more of her today."

She would have a good long soak, and a think. Then she'd make another pot of tea. When in doubt, have a bath and a cup of tea. She knew the baby would start yelling the minute she went through the door, but she still shut it firmly. Then she locked herself in the bathroom. There were now two closed doors and the running taps between her and the baby.

Prill had been watching Oliver closely. He obviously couldn't stand it when Alison cried. For a while he stared at her intently, his face white and tense, his strange, large eyes goggling, then he stood up suddenly, unstrapped her from the high chair and took her in his arms.

"I hate it when she cries, Prill, I just can't stand it," he whispered, walking round and round the kitchen table, making soothing noises. His shoulders were shaking. Prill looked at Colin but he just shrugged in embarrassment.

She went up to them. His face was hidden against Alison's sticky babygro, but she knew he was crying. "Oliver, don't. It's all right, honestly. She cries a lot sometimes. Don't get upset."

"I can't bear it somehow."

"Look," Colin said, trying to be practical. "We've got these now, this stuff may do the trick." But nobody believed him. He didn't believe it himself.

To everyone's surprise Alison had stopped crying. She began making little cooing noises and pulling at Oliver's hair. "Huh, she won't shut up for me," Colin said enviously. But he was glad really. Oliver went up half a notch in his estimation, he was gentle with Alison.

They all sat round the table with the baby on Oliver's knee. He rubbed his eyes. "I think your mother should take her to a hospital," he said firmly.

Prill was shocked. "But why, Oll? What could they do? Don't you think it's just a mood she's in? I mean, she's not got a high temperature, and she's eating."

"I think she may be starving."

"Oh, come on, that's just ridiculous," Colin exploded.

"No it isn't," Oliver said patiently. "There is an illness, I don't know what it's called and it's very rare, when whatever you eat doesn't do you any good. It's something to do with your blood and things. You just lose weight, and—"

"And what?"

"What happens if they can't get you better?" Prill asked anxiously.

"You die."

"Oh, how on earth can that be right?" Colin was shouting. "How on earth do you know that?" But he was frightened.

Oliver was maddeningly calm. "Don't forget my mother was a nurse. She's treated all kinds of people. When she worked on the intensive care unit at St Thomas's—"

"Yes, well, don't let's go into that," Colin said curtly, "you've said enough for one day."

Prill was looking at Alison. "You've certainly done the trick with her, Oll, she's actually smiling."

He was pleased. "Do you think she likes me?" He didn't

seem to notice how she was bending his fingers back, or making a wet patch on his knees.

"Seems to." In spite of everything, Prill was feeling better. They had misjudged Oliver, saying he was babyish, having quiet sniggers behind his back. Just in these last few minutes he seemed to have come over to their side. If her mother did go off tomorrow to find another doctor, it was reassuring to think of Oliver being there. The thought of it actually comforted her.

Chapter Thirteen

IT WAS VERY hot when they went to bed, but there was thunder around and no one could sleep. Colin and Prill lay sweating under damp sheets, and all the doors and windows were open to bring the temperature down. Oliver was in his usual cocoon of bedding, breathing steadily, with his face to the wall. Colin envied him, not knowing he was wide awake listening to Alison crying.

They were all hungry. Prill had brought nothing back from Mooneys' Stores so Mrs Blakeman had made do with what was left, three very small eggs, a heel of bread, and the rest of the frozen chips. After that there were two wrinkled apples to share out. Colin was ravenous. He'd always said it looked disgusting but he really believed he could have eaten a jar of Alison's baby food. The only other food in the house was dog meat, about a dozen tins of it, in one of the kitchen cupboards. Because of Jessie's lack of interest the supply was going down extremely slowly.

Oliver wasn't thinking about meals. Under the bedclothes his hands were clapped over his ears again, anything to muffle the baby's crying. It could never have been as bad as this before. Auntie Jeannie was forever getting up, walking about with her and going back to bed again. He did feel sorry for her.

At one in the morning a storm broke over the bungalow. The thunder was ear-splitting and as it rolled and crashed over the sky the baby cried quite hopelessly, and louder than ever. Prill didn't like storms either and the rain was coming into her room. She got up and closed the windows. The lightning was like an arc lamp, splashing the small field with a second's jagged light before it plunged her back into the hot, airless dark.

The field was empty. The picture of that wasted, ragged creature clawing soil into her mouth then wordlessly screaming at her, close at hand, was carved deeply into Prill's memory. But Father Hagan could be right. She did have a vivid imagination; Mrs Pollock was always telling her that in English lessons. Perhaps that, and the feverishness, and something she'd read... But Prill could no longer distinguish between what she actually saw and heard and the strange tricks her mind was playing on her. So much had happened.

The baby's pain was real enough. They were all awake and they all heard it. As the storm raged over their heads, that voice said everything. Their fear was in it, and their pain, and

Chapter Thirteen

their sense of loneliness. Oliver found it unbearable. He felt he might suddenly get up and quietly strangle Alison if she didn't stop crying, and yet he wanted to comfort her too. It was the most heartrending cry he had ever heard.

When daylight came Colin got up first, feeling very light-headed. It was the effect of sleeplessness and very little food. Instinctively he made his way to the kitchen for something to eat, but someone was there already. The door was open a crack, and he could hear noises.

Something told him not to burst in so he nudged the door open with his foot. He could hear Alison growling bad-temperedly. "Na... na..." she was moaning, and pushing a spoon away from her mouth. Then he heard his mother's voice. She was crying.

Colin stepped back. He'd only seen her in tears once before, when Grandpa Blakeman died; they had been very fond of each other. Now he was appalled, not because he thought mothers had no right to cry, but because of what it meant, here, in this strange house, all on their own, without his father.

She had become a different person in the last few days. Dad was the moody one, given to fits of bad temper and the occasional rage. Mum was much calmer. She always coped in a crisis.

But now she was withdrawing from them; she seemed unable to make her mind up about anything. One minute she was all for getting Dad back, the next she was off the idea and seemed perfectly happy to stay where she was. All yesterday she had sat in the kitchen while Alison screamed the place down, waiting for a hopeless doctor who may, or may not, turn up. There was a limpness about her. It was almost as if she was past caring.

Colin went back to his bedroom, pulled some clothes on, and crept outside. But she heard the front door click. "Where are you going, Colin?" she called out. "It's only half past six."

"I thought I'd walk into Ballimagliesh. I'm going to see if there's another doctor around, someone who could look at Alison. I'll find someone to take you to his surgery. Perhaps someone runs a taxi service. They often do, in remote places like this. I'll buy some bread and stuff, if anywhere's open."

She didn't try to stop him. He just heard an expressionless, "Oh, all right. I hope you won't be gone too long though." That was odd in itself, she would normally have cross-questioned him about how far it was, and whether he had enough money. She would have told him not to thumb lifts.

He was going to do that anyway, if anything came along, but the road was empty. In the distance, under some big trees, he saw two small figures silhouetted against the pale sky, their arms thrust out into the road. When Colin walked past them they stuck out their hands aggressively, almost as if they were trying to get hold of him.

"Don't think we'll be lucky, do you?" he said. "Shanks's pony, I should think, all the way to the village." But they didn't reply; they just opened and shut their mouths at him, and yet no words came out. Funny folk, he thought, and something about the way they stood there made him shiver slightly. But he hadn't got time to stop and talk to them, he had to get to Ballimagliesh.

At eight o'clock Prill and Oliver faced one another across the kitchen table. Between them they had managed to weigh the baby on the bathroom scales. First Mrs Blakeman had stood on them with Alison, then she'd given her to Prill and weighed herself again. Oliver had made them do everything twice and written the figures down in a notebook.

She wasn't the kind of mother who kept neat photo albums or baby books, but she did know what Alison should weigh, and according to Oliver she'd lost half a stone. "She can't have lost that much," said Prill. "Seventeen take away three...then from that you deduct..." he muttered, doing rapid mathematics. "Oh, do shut up, Oll," Prill said. "We don't need all those facts and figures."

He really was peculiar. Last night he'd been so lovely with Alison, calming her down when nobody else could. Now, with these brisk calculations, he was frightening her mother to death. How could he be so thick-skinned?

Mrs Blakeman had already packed a suitcase and a bag of baby things. She came into the kitchen with her coat on, and Alison stuffed under one arm like a parcel. She said quietly, "Of course, now we're going to see another doctor she's decided to calm down. She's like Jessie, contrary. Listen to her, guzzling that biscuit!"

It was reassuring to hear Jessie crunching away again, but the two children were concentrating on Alison. She may have stopped griping but she looked dreadful. Her pink baby chubbiness had gone and there was an unhealthy transparency about her skin. Her face had shrunk somehow; she looked more like a little old man than a young child.

Mrs Blakeman stood by the window watching out for Colin. They'd had nothing to eat yet, and Oliver's stomach was rumbling, so was Prill's. "Is there any breakfast?" she said.

"I found some tins in the back of a cupboard. You could open those. There are some tomatoes, I think, and those baked beans with sausages. I don't want anything."

Her voice was toneless and flat. She didn't even turn round to look at them. It was as if what strength she had left, after the sleepless days and nights, had all been sucked into Alison. There was nothing left over for them.

"Come on, then," Oliver said. Tinned tomatoes were his chief hate, baked beans a close second, but they had to eat something or they'd all be ill. He started getting saucepans out. "By the time these are ready, Colin may be back. Hope he's got some bread."

The day was muggy and quite dark, and all the kitchen lights were on. Oliver bustled round, filling the electric kettle and turning on rings. Then there was a loud click and everything went off together. "Oh *no*! Not an electricity cut. I wonder if it's just the fuse? If I knew where the box was I could probably—" Then Mrs Blakeman said, "Here's Mr O'Malley." She didn't seem to notice about the electricity.

The farmer looked unusually smart in a speckled tweed suit, a new hat and highly polished shoes. "I just came to tell you about the power," he said. "Last night's storm did a lot of damage, there are lines down all over. The electricity board's on with the repairs already, to be sure, and that's why the supply's off. It'll be back on this afternoon, about five, I'm thinking." He flicked a cotton thread off his suit and pulled his tie straight. "We'll not be here ourselves; we're away for the next couple of days. Got to go down into Galway. Donal usually keeps an eye on the place for us. We go every year, about this time. We've got family down there."

Prill stared at him and words formed silently. "Please don't go," she wanted to say. "Please don't shut up your friendly farmhouse and leave us at the mercies of that smelly old man. Please don't leave us here." Instead she said coldly to Oliver, "That's our breakfast finished then. We can't even heat those pans up now."

Mr O'Malley saw the empty tins on the table and listened to Oliver explaining that there was no food in the house. "This won't do at all," he said cheerfully. "I'll send Kevin straight down with something, so I will. And how are you for the milk?"

"We've not got any," Mrs Blakeman said. It was the first time she'd spoken. "I had to throw yesterday's away last night. It was off again; it had turned almost solid. I think the dog drank some of it too. It was sick." She hadn't told the children about the milk, that frightened Prill, so did her voice. It had a dangerous edge to it, it was barbed, not like her mother's voice at all.

John O'Malley turned pink and glanced at the big red

setter as it crept back under the table. It had a biscuit in its mouth but its eyes were glassy and its coat dull. If it was his dog he'd get the vet to it. "Jesus, Mary and Joseph, I don't know what Donal's playing at these days. I'm very sorry, missus, indeed I am. I'll speak to him." He paused. "Er, there's a vet in the village. His name's Keen. Get him to have a look at the dog, if you're worried." He looked at his watch. "We're going soon but the boy'll be right down with some food. Don't want you to go hungry." He smiled rather nervously and tugged at his collar. He was annoyed about the milk. Donal Morrissey was too old to help in the dairy. He'd have found someone else years ago, if it hadn't been for his wife Eileen.

Colin passed the farmer on his way down the track. The old blue pick-up bumped past him shedding bits of straw. It was about as respectable as the "taxi" he'd found in Ballimagliesh.

The only sign of life in the village had been the string of fairy lights above Danny's Bar. Inside he'd found someone sitting behind the counter, eating breakfast.

"Come in, come in do," a voice shouted. "You'll be from the bungalow? And how's the little baby now?" It seemed that everyone knew everything in Ballimagliesh. Mary Malone ran Danny's Bar. She was seventy, very short, and weighed seventeen stone. She was tucking into a huge plateful of bacon and potato cakes. Colin's mouth watered. He mustn't go back without food, but first to business.

She wiped her mouth as he explained what he wanted,

then said placidly, "Young Danny'll take her, don't you worry. He's a driver. He does trips when there's nothing else on. I'll speak to him now."

There was a telephone on the bar counter. She picked the receiver up. Things were clearly arranged so that she only walked about when strictly necessary. "Where is he?" Colin said.

"Upstairs in his bed, if I know anything. *Danny!*" she bellowed. "Get down here, will you! There's a boy here, his mother wants to go to Sligo General. Their baby's sick. Move yourself."

She scrubbed at her plate with a piece of bread. "He'll be down. He'll get your mother to Sligo. Might have to get the car filled up first, might take a while, it's early yet. Would you like to wait here?" Suddenly all the lights went off. "Oh, Jesus Mary, wonder how long we'll be off this time? Danny won't like missing his rashers and potato, I'm thinking."

Kevin O'Malley left a basket outside the bungalow door and went away. His parents were in the pick-up, having words about Donal Morrissey. Dad thought the lady was quite angry about the milk and Kevin didn't want to speak to her. The basket contained fresh milk, two new loaves, and a cake his mother had made for Aunt Mary in Knockferry. He'd been looking forward to a bit of that himself.

Colin brought the basket in with him. As soon as she saw him his mother picked up the suitcase, grabbed Alison, and pushed past him into the hall. "Did you find anyone?"

"Yes. At the bar. It was the only place open, but there's a man there who drives a taxi in his spare time. He's coming. He was still in bed so I started walking back. I thought he'd have caught up with me on the road. Anyway, she says Sligo's the nearest place with a hospital, she said go there."

"But why isn't he here, Colin? Why won't anybody help us?" She sounded peevish, like a spoiled little girl. Colin opened his mouth irritably, then shut it again. She must be much more worried than any of them had realized. It had been far worse for her than anyone else, all those hours alone with Alison. He said quietly, "I'm sure he'll be here soon, Mum. He had to get petrol. Don't worry."

He left her at the front door, staring stonily up the track, and went into the kitchen. Oliver was sitting at the table looking into Eileen O'Malley's basket. His face was colourless. He said in a whisper, "Colin, I just don't believe this."

"What's up, Oll? You look like a sheet." But he knew, even as he said it. There was that mustiness in the atmosphere again, and a sharp, bitter smell he'd met once before.

"I can't believe it," Oliver stammered again. "Honestly, I can't. But look, and she only made these this morning. They were going to take them to Galway or something."

The two brown loaves were spongy and soft, and a green furriness was spreading over them, like hair. In angry panic Colin plunged his arm into the basket and brought the cake out. It was a crumbling, sodden mess, sticky in his hands, and gave off the smell of sickly, over-fermented beer. The milk was in two bottles, but the green foil tops were swollen and cracked across, as if the contents had turned to grey ice.

Now Oliver knew, and was part of it with them. Now he too had heard the baby crying in the night and felt the unnatural heat. Here in his hands was decay itself. His busy brain ached as he tried to find comforting explanations for all that had happened. But he found none.

Colin thought he heard someone coming down the hall. He grabbed the basket. "It's Prill. The taxi's here. Look, I'll do the explaining, Oll. Don't let's frighten her. I'll get rid of this lot right now."

He took everything outside and Oliver heard glass smashing inside a dustbin. He stayed at the kitchen table staring down at a brown pool of foul-smelling liquid that had oozed out between the mesh of the basket.

Chapter Fourteen

"YOUNG DANNY" WAS fifty if he was a day, little, fat, bald, and cheerful like his mother. Colin felt comforted as he helped Mum and Alison into the car. The baby was actually asleep but the minute she woke up she would probably start yelling, and Mrs Blakeman would need someone to talk to on the journey. It was a long way to Sligo and the ancient car couldn't have a top speed of more than fifty. Under all the rust it was probably held together with Sellotape.

Mrs Blakeman promised to try and phone them. Failing that, she would leave a message at Danny's Bar, and she said she would ring Dad, too. Colin was in charge, and they were not to worry. She was sorry to leave them on their own but they couldn't all go to Sligo. Anyway, she could well be back by tomorrow night.

All this was delivered in a flat monotone. She wasn't really interested in them any more, she just wanted to get away. Prill hugged her fiercely but she almost pushed her out of the way as she shut the car door. It was like touching someone asleep, or dead.

Prill ran up the track after the car and watched it turn right towards Ballimagliesh. The two children, in their peculiar tasselled shawls, were standing right in the middle of the road with arms outstretched. Their fingers spiked the sky like winter branches.

Young Danny couldn't have seen the children because he changed gear, revved hard, and drove straight at them. It was a good road from here to the hill above the village and he may as well pick up a bit of speed.

Prill screamed wildly, "Mum! Mr Malone! Let them get out of the way! You'll run them down! Please, stop! What are you *doing*?" As the car rolled forwards over them she shut her eyes, waiting for the screech of brakes and tyres, for glass shattering, the cries, the bloody mess in the road. But the taxi simply chugged off steadily towards Ballimagliesh, and the quiet of the countryside dropped over her again. When she opened her eyes she could see the two small figures a little farther off, still standing motionless in the middle of the road, their hands stretched out towards her.

She turned her face from them and tore back along the track, stumbling over stones, tripping up in the dusty potholes. She just wanted to sleep, to lie in the darkness till this nightmare world had lost its hold upon them. She couldn't fight it any more.

When she got back the two boys were poking about in the hole. She slipped quietly into the kitchen. Jessie was now stretched out full length in the middle of the floor, unnaturally still. She looked dead. In sudden panic Prill dropped to her knees and flung her arms round the big dog's neck, rubbing her cheek against its face. Jessie had been a member of the family for a long time now. How many times had Prill turned to this loyal, utterly accepting creature, when everything was going wrong? How many times had the dog's simple affection given her comfort?

But now she gave a sharp warning growl, and as soon as Prill slackened her arms she stood up and dragged herself away to the other end of the kitchen, as if she was in pain and wanted to be on her own till it had passed.

Prill noticed that she'd only eaten one half of one biscuit. The mess under the table suggested she'd simply played with the rest and spewed them out half eaten. Her bowl of meat was untouched, and it was warm in the kitchen. The stuff was alive with maggots.

Prill's throat tightened. She closed her eyes and turned away. When she opened them again she was looking up at a shelf. There was Dr Donovan's pink juice, untouched, almost offering itself to her. The label prescribed two teaspoonfuls for babies under one. Prill was nearly twelve. She found a soup spoon and swallowed four doses. It might just give her a few hours' sleep, at worst it would make her feel sick, and that would be nothing new.

She crept into her bedroom, closed the window, and

Chapter Fourteen

pulled the curtains across. It was hot again, but she was past caring. She took off all her clothes and lay sweating under a single sheet, praying that sleep would come.

Outside, Oliver and Colin were arguing about something. Prill closed her eyes. She felt pleasantly drunk and quite sleepy. She would definitely drift off now. She hoped she would never wake up.

Colin was soon pedalling along the road on Kevin O'Malley's bicycle. It was one of two he'd found in the farmer's tin garage. On his back was a small rucksack with Dr Moynihan's flashlight in it, and some food he'd bought in the village.

He was going back to the Yellow Tunnel, but this time he wanted to explore it from the top end. A framed map of Ballimagliesh and district that hung in the hall of the bungalow showed a footpath running from behind Ballimagliesh Church across the fields to the old chapel. He might have another look round the ruins before going down the tunnel again.

Oliver was an obstinate pig. His precious hole was quite big enough now and he was making a mess with the soil, but he still wanted to carry on digging. Perhaps he thought he was really a rabbit. He was crazy.

Colin hadn't managed to persuade him to leave off. He'd obviously stopped bothering about what was "allowed", anyway. Prill had gone off to bed and stuck a notice on her door that said "Do not disturb", so perhaps it was as well that someone had stayed behind. At least she wouldn't wake up and find nobody around; and she quite liked Oliver now. They'd be all right together till he got back.

He sat by the little pool in the chapel ruin munching an apple and swigging milk. The food tasted great in the open air, miles away from that bungalow, and he ate nearly all the biscuits before stuffing the packet back into the rucksack. They should all have come really, it was better out here.

There was one thing to do before going down the tunnel. As well as a penknife he'd brought some pan scourers from the kitchen. It was some minutes before he found what he was looking for, the mouldering, mossy headstones all looked much alike, but at last he located it, knelt down, and set to work.

He rubbed away for a good half hour and by the end his fingers were bleeding and his hands raw. The tombstone must be three quarters buried, what he could see was only the top. It was rounded and the design was clearly visible now, a smiling skull with bones crossed underneath and angel heads flanking it at each side. In large Roman capitals was the single word "MORRISSEY" and a date, 1751.

Colin was puzzled. Mrs O'Malley had told them that Donal Morrissey was from County Donegal. He had come to Ballimagliesh as a young man and been taken on as a labourer on her father's farm. She could still remember the stories he used to tell her about his grandmother Bridget who'd been widowed young and brought up eleven children in Kilmacrenan.

Colin stood back and looked at the stone from a distance.

Chapter Fourteen

Now the daylight fell sideways on the lettering, making it sharper. MORRISSEY. There was absolutely no doubt. He tried to think what had happened in history in the year 1751 but couldn't think of anything. Yet it was nearly a hundred years before the Famine. And there was something else odd, too. In those days only the rich people could have afforded gravestones. The poor had planks of wood or were simply buried under mounds of earth.

Bridget Morrissey must have been very poor, left single-handed on a tiny farm with all those children, and anyway, that was much farther north, in Donegal. Donal Morrissey was ending his days in a tumbledown caravan, living on charity from the O'Malleys. He could never have been a rich man either, so it couldn't be the same family.

Ten minutes later Colin was down in the tunnel. The part that had intrigued him was at the top end where it widened out, and where the rocky ceiling had developed a split. Looking up you could see grass waving and a piece of sky.

The storm had turned everything underfoot into mud. He squelched about shining his light over the rocky walls. The place smelt foul and was choked with litter. This was where the village kids congregated in the summer. They had carved initials all over the soft yellow rock.

Just above his head there was a long ledge. He scrambled up on to it, the soles of his sneakers adding grey, rubbery skid-marks to the dozens already there. It seemed there was nothing new to discover; he just found sweet papers and more initials, "Sean loves Mo. True. Very True.", "Daniel L. =

Pauline B." and "Kenny Boyce Rules OK." What a let-down.

The ledge was quite wide, at a pinch you could sleep on it. Colin lay down. He couldn't see the sky any more because the rock jutted forward and blotted out the light. He closed his eyes. For the first time in days he was cool, the dampness of the walls was seeping into his clothes and a mouldy smell filled his nostrils. He might be a corpse, lying there.

Over his head, through layers of earth and stones, he could hear thunder muttering again. What if a great storm blew up and filled the crack with mud, so he couldn't get out? He could die here and nobody would know. He opened his eyes and grinned. He was getting like Prill.

He shone the flashlight directly over his head. Even here someone had been busy with a red felt-tip pen. "I love Rosanna O'Shea," he read, but the letters were very wobbly. It wasn't easy to write with your hand bent back at a horrible angle. Whoever loved Rosanna must be very determined.

Then he saw something else, bits of thin, spidery writing scratched into the rock. It was shaky copperplate script, the old-fashioned kind they'd been made to copy in First Year Juniors. "They shut the way through the woods," he remembered writing laboriously, and "The Lord is my Shepherd".

Some of it consisted of sets of initials. "C.H.M." he made out and "T.M.'48". Next to them, in a bigger hand, was the name "Rachel". Under this the scratching was much fainter. "Lord Have Mercy" was written quite small but with the capital "L" elaborated with wavy lines, and next to it, "Pray for us now and in the hour of our death". All round the bits of writing, in a kind of frame, someone had scratched the word "Salvation", over and over again.

Chapter Fifteen

WHILE PRILL SLEPT and Colin was flat on his back in the Yellow Tunnel, Oliver was digging steadily and feeling a bit uncomfortable about what he'd told Colin. He didn't really want to make the den any bigger, there were other, more important reasons for going on now.

The soil in the middle of the den, in the "hole within a hole", was quite easy to move because it was finer than the rest. There were no hard clods, it was more like sand. It was here he'd found the silver thing and the shreds of silk, and a lot more pottery too, since then. He'd cleaned it all carefully and put it in a polythene bag. This was the place to dig.

The black plastic rubbish sack was getting quite heavy and he'd dragged it out from the bushes to have it near him. The bones and pieces of wood inside weighed quite a lot, and it saved him the bother of climbing in and out all the time.

Chapter Fifteen

The sky had been thickly overcast all morning and now Oliver felt a slight breeze on his face. It was getting quite dark and he could hear thunder in the distance. As he looked down into his den a large raindrop plopped on to his neck, followed by several more. Soon it was raining quite heavily, turning the freshly dug earth into thick mud.

Oliver threw his spade aside, scrunched the mouth of the black sack together, and weighted it down with a brick. That was the end of digging for today. But before going in he glanced back. The pelting rain was washing away at his careful excavations quite rapidly. The simple force of water was much more effective than anything he could do.

The rough hole was rapidly turning into a pit of mud. Puddles had formed in the bottom and the water splashed into them. As Oliver stared down something was happening, something that made him forget all about the cold water streaming down his neck, and the filth sloshing over his sneakers.

Shapes were edging up out of the mud. At first they looked like the remains of trees, a mess of lopped branches flung down the hole in a heap. Some had rough knobs on the end and one was oddly patterned, a main stem with pieces curving out from it, like the teeth of a huge comb. As the rain lashed harder the branches turned pale brown, then yellowish, and something on its own was gleaming perfectly white, like an overturned saucer.

Oliver opened his mouth and tried to breathe deeply. He couldn't, neither could he swallow. It was as if a great lump of gristle had stuck halfway down his throat. Fear rose and washed over him. First he was hot and tingling, then he was icy cold. His mouth felt dry, like paper.

He slithered down into the hole and tried to get his hands under the saucer thing, but it wouldn't move, so he dug his fingers right down, trying to work out how deeply it was buried. It was hard, solid and quite narrow. Then one finger went into a hole. Oliver plunged the other hand up to the wrist in mud and got hold of the thing from underneath. Then he pulled hard.

It resisted for a moment, then shifted. He tightened his grip and pulled again, leaning back on his heels so that he could use all his weight to free the thing. It came quite easily then. The mud made a soft plopping noise and closed up again.

Oliver was no sitting in his hole plastered with mud. Aunt Phyllis's scrubbed, combed little boy was totally un-recognizable. Every inch of flesh that showed looked as if someone had painted it with grey emulsion.

He was staring at the thing in his hands. It was only small, about the size of a small melon, but the child couldn't have been so very young, it had all its adult teeth; he noticed that they were quite perfect. He ran his hands over the skull and turned it over. At the back, just at the base of it, his fingers felt shreds of hair.

Then something inside him snapped suddenly. He felt as if a giant boot had kicked him hard in the stomach and a spasm of pain jerked him to his feet. He flung his arms out,

Chapter Fifteen

still holding on to what he'd found, and was violently sick in the mud.

"When in doubt, have a bath." Auntie Jeannie was always saying that; it was one reason he liked her. She wasn't rigid about when you did things, not like his mother. At home it was *bath* – seven o'clock sharp; *wash hair* – Fridays; *cut toenails* – Mondays. On and on and on.

He needed a bath now to get the mud off, calm himself down, and warm up. He was feeling cold for the first time since coming to Ballimagliesh and as he climbed into the bath his teeth were chattering. He didn't stay in it very long, the water was lukewarm and made him feel shivery. Then he remembered the electricity supply was off. This might be the last hot water for a long time. The house was getting colder.

He tried to wake Prill but she was fast asleep. He had peeped round the door and heard very deep breathing and the occasional snore. He'd given her a shake. "Prill, *Prill*. There's something I've got to tell you," he'd whispered. But she just wouldn't wake up.

There was an awful smell in the kitchen. Vomit. Oliver almost stepped into the yellow pool as he went across the floor to open a window. The dog had been sick again.

She'd obviously tried to eat her dinner then sicked it up almost at once. She was back under the table, her nose buried in her great paws, but her eyes were open and staring at him lifelessly. He felt sorry for her. His mother wouldn't let him have a pet because of the old people, and this dog had frightened him at first, she was so noisy and wild. But his two cousins adored her, especially Prill. Perhaps he could find that vet in Ballimagliesh and get him to come.

He found a mop and bucket in the utility room and sloshed soapy water over the kitchen tiles. He'd watched his mother clear messes up, nurses were used to it. She was always very businesslike and so was Oliver. If you worked quickly you could just about stop yourself throwing up.

When the floor was clean he threw Jessie's food away and filled the bowl up with fresh water. He even patted her gently and she turned pleading eyes on him. Her dumb helplessness made Oliver want to cry. He must find that vet.

Before going out he left a note on the kitchen table. "Gone to Ballimagliesh. Will bring some food back. Oliver." Nothing about what he had found in the muddy pit. Outside he pulled Kevin O'Malley's piece of corrugated iron down into the hole, covering everything up. Prill wasn't likely to go poking about in this weather, but he wanted to be there if she spotted anything.

He had planned to borrow Kevin's racer, he could go fast on that. But it wasn't there. Colin had obviously beaten him to it. He looked in dismay at the machine that was left, an ancient lady's bicycle with a wicker basket fixed in front. It must weigh a ton. Still, the basket was useful. He placed the small package for Father Hagan in the bottom of it and pushed the old bike to the end of the track.

Chapter Sixteen

IT WAS THE wildest day Oliver had ever known. In a different mood he would have felt exhilarated, bowling along the empty road with the rain lashing down, and the huge wind flattening everything in sight as it sent huge branches skittering across his path, and all the time the distant thud of thunder, like gunfire. But after what had just happened the great gale unnerved him. As he battled with the wind he had one picture in his mind, the pattern of white on black that the water had picked out as it poured into the pit. The terror of that moment was in this storm, it was wrapped round his mind like a black cloth, and he couldn't get free of it.

He must tell Father Hagan. Who else was there? The phone was still dead and the O'Malleys had gone away. There was no smoke coming from Donal Morrissey's chimney, and the boy sensed anyway that the old man was weary and wanted to be on his own.

He pedalled hard through the village, lights were on here but there was nobody in the street, it was too wild now. The priest lived at the end, he remembered, near the shop.

It was a great relief to see Father Hagan's old bicycle propped against the kerb outside his house, but nobody came to the door. He banged three times and waited, then he peered through the letter box. There was no light on inside though the next door house was all lit up, as if it was winter.

He walked round to the back and saw an empty garage with its door wide open. So the priest couldn't be in Ballimagliesh at all. Oliver rattled the door handle but it was locked, so he sat down on the kitchen step and stared at the little garden. It was still pouring with rain, a gale was blowing and he was soaked to the skin. But he didn't even notice.

After a few minutes he took a notebook and pencil out of his anorak pocket and began to write something. The letter took a long time. It was hard to know just how much to tell Father Hagan and Oliver still hoped he might come back. But nobody disturbed him as he sat writing laboriously on the cold step.

He folded the piece of paper in two and half pushed it under the door, then he found a stone to put on top of it so nothing could blow it away. Finally he took the package from his bicycle basket. He had wrapped the skull in newspaper then put it in a plastic carrier bag. He looped the handles round the door knob and left it there, gently swinging.

It was easier going back because the wind was behind him,

but he was starting to panic. He'd not forgotten Jessie but if he stopped now, to look for the vet, he might find himself pushing the bike back down that lonely road. If the sky got much darker he'd need lights, and the bicycle didn't have any.

The tin of soup he'd bought at the shop rolled about the wicker basket. It was only when he'd come to pay for his trolley of groceries that he realized he had left all his money at the bungalow. He had found two coins in his pocket to pay for the soup. And he was so hungry. Perhaps Colin would bring a lot of food back.

He was glad when he'd gone over the hill and was on the flat again, past those trees. The two huge elms stood like lonely giants in a landscape where everything else was wizened and twisted by the prevailing wind from the sea. One tree was very rotten and a large branch had been torn off and flung into the road. The other leaned horribly, wheezing and groaning like an old man.

Oliver did not hear it fall. The wind was pounding in his ears as he pedalled towards the bungalow, conscious only of his own heart thumping and the ache in his legs. But if he had looked round he would have seen that the trunk blocked the entire road and that a farm gate in a hedge had been turned to matchwood by the great branches. Ten minutes later and he could have been underneath them.

Father Hagan didn't get back to Ballimagliesh till eight that night. He took the note and the plastic bag inside and didn't look at them till he had made himself some tea and listened to a news bulletin on the radio. His housekeeper, Mrs O'Rourke, was away in Killarney, visiting her sister. She went at the same time each year. Neighbours were very good when the priest was on his own. They brought meals in to him and left food on his doorstep when he was out. This was probably a loaf from Mrs Moffatt next door. He took everything into his tiny sitting-room, and sat down.

"Dear Father Hagan," he read. "Please could you come? The baby is so ill that my aunt decided to go to a hospital with her. Young Danny (from the bar) has driven her to Sligo. We are on our own at the bungalow. Colin and I have been digging a den where they are going to build a garage. I think I may have come across something important, but I'm not sure. Could you come and have a look? One thing I found was the skeleton of a big dog, but I'm not certain about *this*. (Here he had drawn an arrow pointing up to the kitchen door handle.) My cousin Prill is ill too; she keeps having nightmares and feeling sick. I don't feel very well either. Please could you come? Yours sincerely, Oliver Stanley Wright. P.S. If you *could* come we would all be pleased. P.P.S. We think the dog's got a bug. It keeps vomiting."

The priest read the letter again very slowly, noting that the boy had made four separate requests for him to go to them. He stood up and put his car keys in his pocket, glancing over the note again. He didn't take the bit about the digging very seriously, small boys were often very self-important about their treasures.

Then he unwrapped the newspaper and placed the skull

Chapter Sixteen

in front of him, turning it over and over in his hands. He peered into the black eye-sockets, his fingers trembling. When the telephone rang in the hall he jumped violently and almost dropped it.

The line sounded as if a blizzard was blowing down it. The person at the other end was yelling, but Father Hagan could only make out the odd word and asked the caller to repeat everything. It was David Blakeman phoning from Dublin. He had been asked to go to some hospital, it was an emergency; his baby daughter was ill and he was going to his wife. He wanted Father Hagan to look in on the three children, if he was round that way. They would both feel happier if someone could check up on them. He was very sorry to cause trouble and he would phone again tomorrow.

"How is the baby?" Father Hagan shouted back. He thought he heard, "Rather ill, I'm afraid. They want us both to be there."

"Don't worry about the children, I'll make sure—" he began, more quietly, but the line had gone completely dead. He waited in case the phone rang again, but nothing happened, so after ten minutes he set off in his car for the Moynihan bungalow.

Half an hour later he was back at the house. A road block had been set up with cones and flashing lights and nobody was allowed through. A farmer, John Ryan, was arguing with the Garda about the tree. Everyone knew that it should have been felled months ago. It was a mercy no one had been killed.

Father Hagan had turned his car round and driven away quickly. He didn't want to be drawn into any arguments tonight. They all knew about John Ryan's penny-pinching ways. Why foot a bill for tree-felling, if the council would pay?

Nothing would be done about moving the tree till daylight came, and there was no other road to the bungalow. He picked up his telephone and dialled Dr Moynihan's number. The shrill, unbroken, blaring noise told him the line was out of order. He slammed the receiver down in frustration, went into his sitting-room and relit the fire.

When he read Oliver's note again Father Hagan was frightened. He stared down at the neat handwriting and his finger traced the words, "Could you come?... If you *could* come..." The baby must be really sick if the father had been summoned from his painting commission in Dublin and the mother had gone away to Sligo, leaving the three children alone. They were ill themselves, sickly, unable to eat. Oliver complained vaguely of not feeling "very well", but the girl had told him much more.

They had all felt peculiar since setting foot in the bungalow and they had been throwing food away because it had gone bad in the heat. The warm, muggy weather had affected nobody else as it had the frightened family in that luxurious house, making them bilious, giving them sweaty, sleepless nights, causing the very fields round them to reek of decay. Even the dog was suffering. Father Hagan remembered it – Jessie, the big red setter he'd seen tied to the concrete

Chapter Sixteen

mixer. She was a bit noisy and uncontrolled, but those children obviously loved her dearly. It would be terrible if the poor creature died for want of a few pills. He wondered if he ought to tell the vet.

And there had been dreams too, figures that haunted them; the silent, distracted woman at the girl's window and at the stores; the two beggars at the roadside who had torn at her clothes, like monkeys she'd told him, with hair all over their faces.

For a long time Father Hagan just sat and stared into the fire, thinking about all that had happened to them. Then he got up, took a thick box-file down from the bookcase, opened it and spread out papers on the table. Years ago at university he'd neatly lettered the peeling yellow label, "THE BALLIMAGLIESH EVICTIONS, 1848." It was a piece of local research he'd had to do for his degree. Some of these old newspaper cuttings belonged to Donal Morrissey. He should have given them back.

The priest read far into the night and very slowly the puzzle began to make sense. Bits were locking together like pieces of a jigsaw. Tomorrow there would be phone calls to make, he must speak to his bishop, and visit the Garda, but only after he had been to those three children.

The wind blew at the curtains and spidery shadows danced on the walls, webbing the skull that Oliver had pulled out of the pit. Father Hagan got out of his chair and knelt down. In a way he did not understand these innocent children had unleashed some immense power out of the past;

it had taken them back into years of terrible suffering, making them feel in their own bodies the pains and torments of those long dead. Some force was reaching out to them from the other side of death, touching them, threatening their very lives.

His brain was empty, as if the great storm had blown it clean and he fumbled helplessly for words, unable to put together the barest sentence, to commit them all into safe keeping. He was searching his mind for the simplest of prayers for Colin, Oliver, and Prill. He wanted to ask that this great evil might pass over them, that their father and mother would come home to them again, that the poor dog would recover, and that the baby would not die.

"Give them rest, O Lord," he kept repeating. "Give them eternal rest," and their white, terrified faces floated in front of him as, without knowing why, he uttered for living children words used for the burial of the dead.

Chapter Seventeen

"At least we'll sleep tonight," Colin said. "That's one way to look at it. At least Alison won't be here, to keep us all awake with her yelling."

"How d'you know we'll sleep?" Prill's voice was hard. "Nobody's had a decent night's sleep since we got here. It's been too hot."

"Well, it certainly isn't hot now," Oliver pointed out. "I'm cold. I had a bath before I went to the village and I could do with another."

"You can't," Prill snapped. "You used up all the hot water and the immersion heater's not working now."

"Are you sure?" Colin said. "The electricity was supposed to be coming back on at five. It's seven o'clock now."

"Switch everything on, if you don't believe me."

He went round the house clicking switches. Prill was

right, the supply was still off. "The repairs must have taken longer than they thought," he said. "It'll be back on soon."

But Oliver knew it wouldn't be. There had been lights on in Ballimagliesh and the cottage at the top of the track had been lit up too, as he pedalled by. It was just this house.

They were all shivery. The thunder had petered out but a wind still howled round the bungalow, rattling everything that moved. The temperature seemed to have dropped quite sharply, and they pulled jeans and sweaters on over their summer clothes.

Jessie crept around after the children, whimpering. Now she was anxious to be with them, and whenever they sat down she flopped at their feet. When he stroked her, Colin could feel how bony she was. They'd simply lost count of how much food they'd had to throw away, how many times they'd gone out to the dustbin and emptied her bowl. There were always maggots. Colin saw them but said nothing to Prill. Prill saw them and said nothing either. They all knew they were there, and that it wasn't the heat. Food didn't go off so quickly.

The whole place was beginning to feel damp, even the thick carpets, unbearably warm before to their bare feet, seemed to have moisture in them. "You can't get warm if you have cold feet," Oliver announced firmly, pulling thick socks on. "That's what my mother says, anyway."

They tried to light a fire in the sitting-room with old newspapers and a torn-up carton, but it was hopeless. There was a five-minute blaze then the paper was finished, and the damp cardboard smouldered, filling the room with smoke. Colin brought some twigs in from outside and threw them on half-heartedly, but they were sodden after the rain and wouldn't even light.

"Gave up on the den, did you?" he asked Oliver. "I see you've thrown that piece of sheeting down it."

"Oh well, you know. It started raining and I just thought it would be out of the way, till I could fix it properly." Oliver had turned scarlet. He didn't want the other two to know about the pit, not yet anyway. He wanted to show everything to Father Hagan first.

But Colin didn't notice he was embarrassed. He had a secret of his own, the writing in the tunnel. He'd climbed out of there pretty quickly when the rain started. It wouldn't be so funny getting trapped in a place like that. But he could remember the words quite clearly. "Lord Have Mercy", and "Salvation". What did it mean?

Prill was in a world of her own, too. The pink medicine had made her feel sick when she woke up, and after the long, drugged sleep she had a splitting headache. Nothing was different, nothing was better. She still felt hungry but the very act of eating seemed to turn her stomach. Nobody had been to the house, nobody could telephone, no letters had come. The only thing that had changed was the weather. All afternoon the sky had grown steadily darker and a thick rain had set in. The wind was now flinging it against the glass like gravel.

All three of them had been to the phone in turn and lifted

it up secretly. All three had listened in vain for the reassuring purring sound. There may be a message for them at Danny's Bar but they couldn't go out in this wind. It must be the gale that had stopped Father Hagan getting to them, Oliver decided.

The only thing to do was to go to bed early and walk to Ballimagliesh in the morning. But before getting into bed Prill stuffed some things into a bag. The other two could do what they liked but once she had left this house she did not intend to come back.

The tin-opener was electric so they couldn't open Oliver's can of soup. All the milk had been thrown away so there was nothing to drink but cold water. Colin produced three biscuits and an apple from his rucksack and shared them with Oliver. Prill didn't want anything to eat and went off to bed.

What they ate tasted of nothing, it was like eating thick paper. But the two boys chewed their way through it because it was food and their stomachs were empty. Ten minutes later Oliver went to the bathroom and was violently sick. He said nothing to his cousin but he knew now that it would have been the same with any kind of food. Their own bodies had started to play terrifying tricks on them.

"I'm going to bed," he told Colin. "The sooner we go to sleep the sooner it'll be morning." He was under the covers in twenty seconds flat, kicking off his shoes and scattering clothes all over the floor. It was so unlike Oliver. Bedtime was usually quite a ritual with him.

Chapter Seventeen

Colin lay wide awake in the dark room, hunger squeezing his stomach like a fist getting the last juice out of an orange. The pain was agony. He'd never sleep unless he ate something else. There must be some food in one of those kitchen cupboards.

They'd found candles earlier on, and he'd stuck one in an egg cup and put it by his bed. He got up, lit it, and went down the passage to the kitchen. By its feeble, flickering light he searched through the cupboards and along the shelves but there were only tins that he couldn't open, and packets of flour and rice.

He found some Bonios and a half-eaten tin of dog food and tried chewing a bit of biscuit, washing it down with gulps of cold water. But his throat was horribly dry, and the mealy lumps stuck halfway down his windpipe, hurting him. It was as though he'd tried to swallow a handful of gravel.

The stomach pains were getting steadily worse. He sat in a circle of candlelight at the kitchen table with the can of dog meat in his hand, fingering the old bent spoon Mum had found to dollop it out for Jessie. He sniffed. The meat smelled quite fresh and juicy, rather like stewing steak.

Suddenly his bare feet buried themselves in something warm and soft. He'd forgotten the dog for a minute, fast asleep by the sound of it, slumped under the table. He reached down and pushed the tin in her direction. "Jessie," he whispered. "Come on, girl." But the dog didn't stir. Colin listened more carefully. When the wind dropped for a minute he could hear steady breathing, light and rather quick, like a small child. At least she was still alive.

He sniffed at the tin again, and his stomach creased with pain. It was a punchball with a thousand knotted fists belting it from all sides. He would eat Jessie's food.

He dug the bent spoon right down, and crammed a huge lump into his mouth. He wouldn't breathe in or out while he was eating. That way he wouldn't taste anything. It was food. His tongue pushed it to the back of his throat where it disintegrated into a kind of gritty pulp, but he was determined to swallow it. It would fill his belly and give him a few hours' sleep.

But his throat muscles suddenly seized up completely, he was retching with the meat still in his throat. He got up, knocking the candle over, and groped his way to the sink, where he clawed the dog food out of his mouth, feeling blindly for the taps and turning them both on full.

Water, he must run water. He couldn't see anything but he stood there shaking, listening to the rain as it poured down into the darkness, and the tap water drumming into the sink. He was sick repeatedly, he had never been so sick, and when it was over at last, and his stomach felt tiny and squeezed dry, like a rag, he went on standing by the window listening to the gushing of the tap. Water, he must use water, to clean his mouth and teeth and hands. He splashed it all over his face and let it run over his fingers. Somehow it made him calm again.

At last he leaned forward and switched the tap off. The jets of water in the steel sink sounded quite loud. The others were sleeping. He must go back to bed, warm up, and somehow get to sleep himself. He managed to relight the candle. The tin of dog meat was still on the table with the old spoon beside it, and maggots were wriggling on the rim and on the handle of the spoon where he had smeared it.

He was sure that his cousin wasn't asleep.

"Oll?" he whispered. "Are you awake?"

Oliver grunted. He was trying to ignore the waves of sickness that kept sweeping over him, and doing cycling movements under the bedclothes to get himself warm.

"Don't let's stay here tomorrow. Let's go to Ballimagliesh."

"No, we won't. We'll set off early. But let's try and get some sleep."

"I can't sleep. I'll never sleep tonight."

"Yes you will," the voice in the darkness said, quite bossily. "Make your mind a complete blank, it helps you relax; you'll drop off then. That's what my father always advises anyway, when I can't sleep."

Colin was thinking, If I hear one more word about what your father says, I'll *brain* you. But he just said, "Good night, Oll." He was glad he was there.

Colin heard the noise first. He had been sleeping very lightly and was awake at once. He sat up in bed and listened; apart from the blasts of wind, the panes rattling, and a moan from Jessie in the kitchen, there was quietness.

Perhaps the cold had woken him. He was shivering as he

lay there and dampness was seeping into him. It was in the bedding, the curtains and the floor. The air that touched his face was heavy with it and when he brushed at his cheek in the darkness his hand came away wet. The same dank smell of mouldiness was back in the room, but much stronger than before, and there was a sharpness in it now that clutched at his throat.

As he sat in bed he heard the noise again, and this time he was certain. It was Alison. He recognized the familiar hoarse sobbing. His mother must have come back in the small hours, after they'd gone to bed. A wild hope sprang up inside him... Perhaps his father was here too.

Then the noise stopped abruptly. Colin strained his ears but the sodden darkness held nothing except the noise of the wind and rain, and his own breathing. He lay down again and closed his eyes firmly, willing it to be a dream, begging for sleep to come, bringing day nearer.

Oliver was a quiet sleeper and hardly disturbed the bedclothes once he was comfortable, but tonight his dreams were wild. He was at the bottom of a deep pit and his arms and legs were hopelessly entangled with the limbs of others who lay there quite patiently, staring up at the sky, while earth was thrown in on top of them. It was pouring with rain. Wet soil clung to his hair and stuck to his eyes, making them smart and run, and he was shouting, "Please let us get out, don't bury us yet. Some of us are still alive." But somebody went on shovelling earth over them mechanically, a man with a silly, fixed smile on his round moon face, the face of the priest, but with all the compassion sucked out of it.

He cried again, "*Please*, let us get out, we are not dead," but earth showered down, filling his mouth, and he fell back on to bodies that were already disappearing into the foaming mud. There were screams all round him, women, little children, old men, but as he lay there the sounds faded and the storm drowned the voices until all he could hear was a single cry breaking the darkness, the desolate sobbing of a child.

Oliver opened his eyes and pinched himself. *Alison*, it must be. They were back. But no, they were miles away, in Sligo, unless, unexpectedly… "Colin," he whispered. "Are you awake?" he paused and listened again. "Can you hear it?"

"Yes. It woke me up, too. I thought it was Alison for a minute, then I thought it might be the dog, or that I'd dreamed it, but… *Listen!*"

The noise was much louder now, as if the baby was on the other side of the bedroom wall. The voice was more insistent, sharper. There was great pain in it. Oliver put his hands over his ears. "If they would only go to her," he said. "If they would only comfort her. Why do they leave her alone?"

Colin heard springs squeak as Oliver got out of bed, then sniffling noises. He fumbled about in the darkness, found him, and sat down on his bed with his arm round his shoulders. "Come on, Oll. It'll be all right in the morning. We won't stay here, we'll go to Ballimagliesh. We could stay in the pub till Mum gets back. Listen, it's stopped now, anyway."

But he couldn't lie and say, "You must have been

dreaming," because he'd heard it too. And Prill must have heard it. Colin suddenly wanted to go to her, but even as he was groping about for the candle the quiet was shattered by an almighty scream. It was his sister.

The two boys stood up at the same moment and their heads crashed together. Then they were feeling blindly for the bedroom door, tripping up and banging into one another. It could have been funny, a Laurel and Hardy act with the lights off, but they were both terrified.

At last Oliver found the door and half fell into the hall. Colin clutched at his hand in the darkness and held it firmly. The smell in the bungalow had thickened, it was like dead leaves, and the cold air was wet on their faces.

A gust was banging Prill's bedroom door open and shut. Colin could just see a small, pale figure looking out into the roaring dark. All the windows were wide open and everything was blowing round the room.

"Prill! For heaven's sake – you'll catch your death. Look, you're absolutely sodden!" She did nothing, said nothing, till Colin reached past her to shut the windows. Then she tried to stop him, clawing at his arm like a cat and letting out the sudden, high-pitched squeal that had so frightened them.

"Don't! Oh, don't! We can't breathe if you do that." She thrust her hands out, palms flat against the blackness, as if it was a solid wall. "I can't get out. It's in my throat. Everything's falling… Oh, *please*!" The words stopped suddenly. They heard choking noises and Prill was on the floor, a squirming whiteness in the gloom.

Colin slammed all the windows shut and Prill cried loudly, "Don't, Colin! Don't. How can we get out now?"

"Grab her other arm," he whispered to Oliver. "Don't let go of her. Let's try and get to the kitchen."

Between them they manoeuvred Prill through the bedroom door, but she was a dead weight, and her bare feet slithered along the polished floor. They half dragged, half pulled her along the passage, but she tried to shake them off, shouting wildly that she would not go, that she was suffocating. But when they had lit candles and found jam jars to put them in, and she was sitting at the kitchen table with Colin on one side and Oliver on the other, she became much calmer. She looked round and blinked, staring at their flickering faces with surprised eyes, as if they were complete strangers. Then she laid her face flat on the table and sobbed.

They sat huddled together for a long time, listening to the howling wind and to Prill's helpless crying. Jessie lay under the table, fast asleep. She had not responded to Prill's voice, and she loved Prill best. Normally she'd have growled and jumped up the minute anybody came through the door. But it was as though all her doggy senses were completely dead.

Secretly, Oliver poked her quite sharply with his foot, but the dog didn't move. It was an unnatural sleep, like coma, the lifelessness of someone mortally injured whose life ebbs silently away, unseen. He didn't say anything. Colin knew quite well what was happening to the dog, and if Prill suspected that the poor thing really was near its end she'd go hysterical again. As soon as they got to the village he'd go and find that vet, Keen, while Colin and Prill woke up Father Hagan.

Outside, the wall of dark was slowly lightening. It would be dawn soon. Somehow they must get to Ballimagliesh, but the gale had strengthened. It was as if the narrow, high-hedged track to their door was acting like a funnel; the huge wind poured down it, flinging the debris of fields and lanes at them with the force of bullets. When Colin crept outside to have a look round, the wind almost flattened him.

They were all dressed by six. Prill was ready first and waited in the kitchen, staring out listlessly at the wildness of fields and sky. She hadn't washed or combed her hair, or cleaned her teeth; there was a foul taste in her mouth and her head pounded. But her body was nothing to do with her any more. She didn't care.

"Come on, Prill," Colin said rather nervously. "We've got to wrap up. Look at the weather." He bent over her and did up the buttons of her cardigan. It was Mum's, an old holey thing she wore in bed. "What have you got this on for?" Now he was close to her he could see how sunken her eyes were, and how her skin glistened. It had that awful greenish pallor they'd noticed in Alison.

"You can't go like this. Where's your anorak? It's raining. Where did you—?" She cut him off. "Listen, listen to it. That's what I could hear in the night. It's what woke me. I wasn't asleep. I *knew*." She stood up and grabbed his arms, so fiercely that it hurt. Oliver was standing in the doorway with a jersey half pulled over his head.

The cry of the child was very loud now. Just for a moment it sounded as if she was in the room with them. Then the noise faded, melting into the wind as it howled round the house. They listened and it came again. Now it was thin and far away, now the gale brought it back to them, and it was no longer a child's voice but older and deeper, a low weeping, a voice with all the sadness in it that they had ever felt.

The three children stared at each other, then looked away. They were beyond everything now, beyond hunger, beyond tears. As they stood together outside, trying to keep upright in the teeth of the wind, Colin banged the door shut and double-locked it. Inside, Jessie started howling.

Prill started to cry. "We can't leave her, Colin. It's cruel. I'm going back." She turned round and made for the door. She believed they would never get away from this place, never break free. She wanted to be with Jessie.

The gale howled down the track, almost blowing them over. Stones and gravel were hurled up at their faces, battering them like giant hail. Colin shouted, "Prill, she'll have to stay there for a bit. She's too weak, she'll hold us up. Oliver says he'll go and tell the vet, the minute we get to Ballimagliesh. Oh, *come on*, can't you?"

But Prill stayed where she was, her fingers twisted round the big front door knob, wrenching at it, as if she was trying to pull it off. "I'm not going without her," she sobbed. "Let me into the house. *We can.* I'll carry her."

Colin hesitated and took a step towards the bungalow,

feeling in his pocket for the keys. He'd hated shutting the door on Jessie, and now she was just behind it, howling and scratching pitifully. Perhaps they could—

"*No,*" said a voice behind him and his shoulders were being gripped very tight. "Turn round, walk away from her. It'll take us all our time to get up the track in this wind. I'll deal with Prill. We can't take Jessie, and that's final."

Colin spun round. The voice was unfamiliar, loud, piercing, unnaturally high. It was the voice of someone used to being obeyed. It was Oliver.

He'd pushed Colin away and gone back to Prill on the step. They were fighting. Prill was screaming. "No! *No!* Leave me alone! Why should I do what *you* tell me, you don't understand about Jessie. I've seen you kicking at her, don't think I've not—" She broke off suddenly; there was a sharp crack and Colin saw Oliver strike her very hard across the face.

She was taller than he was, and to get her down off the step he had wrapped both his hands round her arm and was tugging violently. Colin winced, that must be horribly painful. As he watched, she let out an agonized scream. Oliver was clawing and pulling wildly at poor Prill in his efforts to get her away from the bungalow. "Prill," he was shouting. "You must come with me. We must get away from this house. *Trust* me, Prill!"

She was now spreadeagled against the door, staring down at the puny little boy in absolute terror. "No, no," she was moaning, but her voice was less certain, and her body sagged a little, as if her knees were giving way.

Colin came up and stood on the other side. "Come on, Prill," he said quietly. "Oliver's right." He put his arm round her shoulder and helped her off the step. Oliver stepped quickly between them and the house, spreading out his bony hands to the howling wind. But Prill had given in, and she walked away without another word.

Very slowly they inched forwards, clinging together for safety, and at last reached a fork in the track where a narrow path went off into a field, towards the trees near Donal Morrissey's caravan.

Oliver stopped and pulled them all to a halt. "Come on!" Colin shouted, above the gale. "Let's keep on going." He wanted to keep Prill on the move. She was in a state of near hysteria, and if she broke away now and ran back, there would be another struggle. This time she might win.

"This is the way," he heard. "This is the way we must go. He's waiting for us."

It was the same strange, high-pitched voice, a sound so piercing it hurt the ears. And there was such authority in it, such assurance. How could it be the voice of a small boy like Oliver? Colin was frightened. He turned round in the path and looked at him. Prill released her grip on his arm and looked too.

The boy was standing just below them by a broken stile. The overgrown hedge that bordered the field was being blown right over by the wind. He could have crouched under it for shelter. But he stood well away from it, in the middle of the track, his arms thrust out towards them and his head thrown back, almost as if he gloried in the storm.

The face and body were Oliver's, but he was someone they no longer knew. And there was a stillness about him. It was as though they were looking out of darkness towards a steady point of light. The world had gone mad and wild; land, sea and sky were locked together in a riot of noise. And in the eye of the storm stood Oliver, in that place of peace where all the tumult ended.

"We must go to the old man," he repeated. "He's waiting for us."

Colin and Prill looked at one another. They both knew they had to obey him, but they didn't know why. Why should they turn their backs on the village, on the kindly priest, on the chance of finding a vet for Jessie? Why go instead to a stinking caravan and a crazy old man who'd threatened to set his dog on them? But Oliver had already turned his back and climbed over the stile. And they followed him.

In the open fields it was almost impossible to stand. The landscape was a dirty yellow blur, earth and sky became one as the rain whipped at their faces and made their eyes stream. The sea thundered down below and the copse of stunted trees was flattened like wind-blown hair.

The old blue van rocked gently in the middle of the fields, looking like Noah's Ark. There was a light inside and smoke poured from the chimney. The old man was at his door, looking up at the sky. He whistled for his dog, then he saw the three children. For a second he stood quite still, then shouted to them. But the wind drowned him, so he put his hands to his mouth and called again, beckoning them over.

Very slowly, Colin started walking, but Prill stopped on the muddy path. "Come on, Prill," Oliver said. "The wind's dropped a bit. Let's get under cover while we can. He's waiting for us."

She looked into his eyes, searching for the person she'd once known, the fussy, self-opinionated little boy who'd threatened to spoil their holiday. But that Oliver had gone. "He's waiting, Prill," this boy repeated; his voice was harder now, and his fingers were plucking at her.

This time she didn't snap or make jokes. She didn't say, "You and your old people, you're obsessed with that dirty old man." She simply took the hand he held out to her and followed him across the field.

Chapter Eighteen

THE OLD MAN could see that Colin and Prill were frightened, though the younger boy seemed very anxious to get inside. He held the door open for them. The older ones didn't move, but Oliver's foot was already on the step. "We must go in," he said loudly. "He's been expecting us." But they backed away. In the end Donal Morrissey pulled them inside himself.

The girl looked ill, she was shaking uncontrollably and she was wringing wet. "You," he said roughly, making her sit down in the one armchair by the stove. Put this round yourself, do. Get warm." The smelly blanket he was thrusting at her made Prill's flesh creep, but she didn't dare refuse it. She pulled it round her trembling shoulders. It stank to high heaven but at least it was dry. Very gradually her teeth stopped chattering.

"You boys," he was grunting, pulling more covers from a

bed and spreading them on the floor, "Sit on these. It's food you'll be after now, I'm thinking."

The dog sidled up to them nervously, sniffing them all in turn, then sitting down at Oliver's feet. He touched it gingerly, but he had eyes only for Donal Morrissey, eyes that were now curiously bright, big with expectancy in the light of the smoking oil-lamp. Prill stared at him. He was waiting for something to happen.

Colin was peering curiously round the caravan at the boxes and all the bags of old rubbish. The table was covered with newspapers and ancient books. Old Donal must spend hours poring over them. He analysed the various smells, dog, peat, and some kind of stew. There was a big pan of it, bubbling on the stove.

Prill looked at the old man as he shuffled about. As the wind tore across the fields, the van swayed on its moorings and the gale battered at the thin walls. "Here," he said. "You want warming." She sat up jerkily. He'd pushed a tin bowl into her hand and was ladling something into it, a fatty broth with cabbage strips and lumps of bacon floating on top. When they all had a bowl he fetched a loaf and tore pieces off it. "Dip this in," he said. "You need food inside you."

Prill's stomach heaved. The spoon he'd given her was caked with bits of dried-up food. The soup seemed to consist of grease and old scraps of meat and vegetables. The smell of it made her feel sick. She put the spoon down, trembling in case the old man got angry and forced her to eat. Then, without knowing why, she looked up into his eyes.

Donal Morrissey was staring down at her intently. Suddenly he seemed immensely tall and his eyes burned into her. Prill stared back, as if hypnotized; she knew that face well, all her dreams were about it, bony, gaunt and fleshless. She recognized the domed forehead from which the wisps of hair, once a wild auburn, sprang back. All that had happened to them was in this face.

What was going to become of them now, shut up in this caravan with this strange old man? Her body began to tremble and she pulled the filthy blanket round her more closely, so he wouldn't see. The storm still raged round outside and the van was rocking. Then the wind hurled something down on the roof with a great clatter. The sudden noise was deafening and Prill's hand flew to her mouth, forcing a scream back.

They had not escaped. The terrors of the house had followed them across the wild fields. She would not look through the tiny windows in case she saw the stick woman staring in at her; she would breathe in the smell of the blanket, it was better than the foul, rotten smell of the land.

Donal Morrissey saw her terror and didn't understand. Her brother was shivering too, hunched over the puttering stove, staring up at him out of a wild, white face. The storm was still blowing strongly. They couldn't leave yet. He looked from one to the other. Then he knew what to do; he would show them his treasures.

He pushed a chair over to the stove and sat down next to

Chapter Eighteen

Prill. "See this? That boy brought it. I cleaned it up."

She looked into his cracked palm. "What is it?" she whispered.

He rattled the silver nut against her ear. "Found it, so he says. Dug it up when he was making a hole to play in, outside Moynihan's bungalow. And this too, wrapped round it. Cost money that would. It's silk. Would have rotted otherwise surely. Oh, they were fine folk."

"Who were?" said Colin, edging forward, fingering the silver nut. "Who did these things belong to? Who were these rich people?"

The old man was muttering to himself as the two children examined Oliver's relics. But he never took his eyes off them. He didn't want the tiny things to be dropped. The floor was full of cracks.

"It's a baby's rattle," Oliver said clearly. "The handle's missing, but that's what it is. It's probably got a little stone inside it, to make the noise."

"But where exactly did you find it?" Prill asked. "Did you really dig it up and—"

"And why didn't you tell us?" Colin broke in impatiently. "It could have been very important. Why keep it a secret?"

"It *is* important," Oliver answered calmly. "But I couldn't tell anyone, not straight away. I was waiting."

Colin and Prill exchanged bewildered looks. Why had he waited? Did he mean for this moment? Had he known all along that the night of terror they had just lived through would end here, in this caravan, with Donal Morrissey?

"*Why* keep it a secret?" Colin said again.

"Because sometimes things can't be told, till the right time comes. You've got a secret, too. You must tell him about it."

The two boys looked at one another, and Colin knew that he meant the writing in the tunnel. But how could Oliver know about that? Had he been spying on him? It was impossible.

The old man had fished out other things to show them. "Perfect, this one is, they're the same. See?" He thrust the silver rattle on its carved handle under Oliver's nose, his eyes glittered and his voice was breathy with excitement. "Didn't know I'd got this, did you? Or this? Your bit of silk came from this piece. It was a shawl, I reckon. And look at this, will you? It was her prayer book."

Oliver took the rattle and the square of silk from the old man, looked at them quickly, almost politely, and gave them to Colin. No, he hadn't seen them before, but his face showed no surprise. It was calm, almost self-satisfied. He looked like someone solving a difficult puzzle, methodically, piece by piece; someone very confident, who had no doubt that he could complete it.

Old Donal took the reddish cloth from Colin and spread it over his knees. Then he put the prayer book on top of it. "This was hers. They were all hers, all these things. They'd been kept from the old days and passed on to her."

"Who?" said Prill. "D'you mean your mother?"

The old man opened his mouth but it was Oliver who answered.

"His grandmother. He means his grandmother, Bridget Morrissey. She was born in Ballimagliesh but she went away to live in the north, in County Donegal, when she got married. I'm right, aren't I, Mr Morrissey?"

"Aye, you are, boy. She did so."

He didn't seem at all surprised by what Oliver had said. There was an understanding between them. It was almost as if the boy was willing him to unfold his story, just for the benefit of the other two, but as if he knew the facts already and didn't need to be told.

Donal opened the prayer book and showed them what was written inside. " 'Bridget Morrissey, Ballimagliesh, 1865.' See that? She was seventeen when she wrote that. It's a fine hand, so it is. They could all read and write. That's a hundred years old, that is, but these…older still, these are."

"I don't understand," Prill said flatly. "I just don't understand any of it. Why are these things you dug up so important, Oliver? How does he come to have things like them? And I don't understand about the grandmother. Can't he explain to us?"

Colin exchanged looks with Prill. They both felt certain about one thing now. In these keepsakes they would find the key to all that had happened to them. That was why Oliver had brought them here.

"You lived with her in Donegal, didn't you?" Oliver said to the old man, taking no notice of Prill and Colin. "You didn't leave till you came here, to work on a farm?"

"So I did, but *she*… Well now, she stayed here till she was married. The Morrisseys were Ballimagliesh people, born and bred. Wealthy too, they were, in the old days. There are Morrisseys buried in the Chapel of Our Lady, above Ballimagliesh Strand."

"I know," Colin said. "I found a headstone in the ruins. It had Morrissey on it."

He shot a look at Oliver and the boy's bright, confident eyes looked back, eyes that said, "*I knew*. That was your secret, wasn't it? I was waiting for you to tell him that."

Old Donal thrust his face right up against Colin's. "You've been down the tunnel then, where they were? Those names – it was her told me about those names, Bridget told me, before she died at Kilmacrenan. First thing I did was look for them, when I came to Ballimagliesh. They'd written their names in that hiding place, by the strand. She'd seen them too."

"And it was the same Morrisseys?" Colin said quietly.

"So it was. Ah, the poor souls, no rest for them, no refuge, no one to bury them, all perished." The old man's voice cracked and he stared into the flames of the stove. He seemed to have forgotten the three children. His mind had taken a well-trodden path where nobody, not even Oliver, could follow.

"They died when the harvests failed, didn't they?" Oliver prompted him. "When everyone died?"

"All of them. All the Morrisseys. And no one to bury them. Others were thrown into pits of lime, dozens together, like animals."

"You mean in the 1840s?" Prill said. "In the years of the potato famine?"

"In the great hunger."

Colin and Prill fell silent, but Oliver was strangely excited and stood up suddenly. Without realizing it he'd grabbed the old man by the shoulder. Donal was startled for a second, then he laid his grubby hand on top of Oliver's, and kept it there, as though he wanted comfort.

"There's just one thing I don't understand," the boy said shrilly. "It's all clear to me now, except for one thing."

One thing… Prill and Colin exchanged hopeless looks. They were still totally bewildered.

It seemed that the Morrisseys buried in the graveyard above the Yellow Tunnel were the old man's remote ancestors. In those days they were prosperous. Only the rich would have toys made of silver and wrap their babies in silk. Years later his grandmother's family had died in the famine. They had scratched their names in the rock in that tunnel above the beach.

Oliver had dug things up that he claimed belonged to the Morrisseys, things very like the old man's treasures. Yet he'd found them near the new house, miles away from the Yellow Tunnel.

And Donal Morrissey had just told them that the whole family had perished during the potato blight. So how could they have anything to do with him? This grandmother of his had lived on into ripe old age, moved away, and raised a family.

"It's your grandmother," Oliver was saying. "That's the bit I can't work out." Prill and Colin were reassured. He seemed to know so much, and his knowledge was so particular. He knew things about this place that he couldn't possibly have dug out of his father's history books. Just for a minute they saw the old Oliver, worrying about pernickety details as he bored into the old man's memory like a dentist's drill, determined to find the last piece of the jigsaw.

"You say your grandmother Bridget was born in 1848…"

Donal Morrissey was only half listening. He was getting tired. "Look at that handwriting," he murmured. "She could have been a scholar, so she could."

"But the *date*," pressed Oliver. "You told us she was seventeen in 1865. Now if what you say is true—"

"*True?* Of course it's *true!*" The old man's hand had dropped away from Oliver's shoulder. He was shaking with anger.

But the boy was totally wrapped up in his calculations and didn't even notice. "If she was a baby in the worst years of the famine she was born just about the time when the whole family died. Therefore she couldn't possibly have—"

His voice was cut off abruptly by the dog who got up suddenly, shook itself, and growled. There was a shuffling noise by the door, then someone knocked.

When the old man opened it they saw that the storm was dying down. The high wind was breaking up into a series of fitful gusts; the rain had washed everything clean and blown the clouds up amazingly high, into a calm sky. The air felt quite warm now, but the oppressive heat had gone.

Father Hagan's round moon face was peering in at them very anxiously. The dog jumped up at him and barked, and Donal Morrissey muttered peevishly, "Thanks be to God, Father, you're a stranger surely. Days I've been waiting for you to show your face. I'd got things to show you."

"I'm sorry, Donal. It's only two days," the priest said, "and I tried to come last night, but a tree fell on the road and it's only just been cleared. Jack Ryan's arguing with the council already."

The old man smiled knowingly. "Him… That man is it? I could—"

"Not now, Donal, there's no time now. Show me what it is quickly, will you? I want these children to come back with me. I have something to tell them."

Prill had thought she would never go back to that house but her feet were taking her along the track after the others. When the bungalow came into view it looked so ordinary, so small, with the sun shining on the fresh white paint and the priest's old car slewed sideways by the yellow skip. Colin had run on ahead to find Jessie. Oliver walked by Father Hagan's side, prattling nineteen to the dozen.

Prill followed very slowly with her eyes on the priest as he puffed along the path, with Oliver's black sack humped over one shoulder, like a solemn Father Christmas in mourning.

Chapter Nineteen

MUCH LATER THAT day she sat next to Colin on Dr Moynihan's big sofa with her back firmly turned on what was going on outside. There was a faint, smoky smell from last night's attempts to make a fire, but fresh air blew in through the open window. Oliver sat cross-legged on the floor listening to Father Hagan, with the same bland, all-knowing look he'd had in Donal Morrissey's caravan. Now and again he glanced round at the men outside. Two were in his hole, scraping away with spades; a head popped up occasionally and called someone over. There were also two policemen, an oldish man in a dark suit, and another clergyman, peering curiously down into the mud.

They'd been there all day, brought to the bungalow by the priest's telephone calls, but the children had only just come back from Ballimagliesh. They had had hot baths in Father

Chapter Nineteen

Hagan's little house and Mrs Moffatt next door had made them big plates of eggs and bacon. None of them had been able to eat very much but at least the food had stayed down, and nobody had been sick.

While they were eating, Father Hagan had produced an old file of notes and newspaper cuttings about what had happened years ago in Ballimagliesh. They boys were interested but Prill's head ached. She was feeling a bit better, but the priest's words rang in her head like giant gongs. There were so many of them, so much to take in. And her parents still hadn't phoned from Sligo.

Jessie sat at her feet, very subdued. If the children called to her she half pricked her ears then laid her long nose on the floor indifferently, and when she followed Prill around it was on very wobbly legs. But she'd stopped vomiting, and an hour ago she'd been persuaded to eat a small plate of food. The vet was coming tomorrow to check her over, but the children knew that she was going to be all right now.

"What Oliver has found out there," Father Hagan was explaining carefully, "was probably their last hiding place—"

"It was called a scalpeen," interrupted Oliver. "It was just a big hole, roofed over with twigs and stuff."

The priest was talking about the Morrisseys, a family that had been well-to-do in the old days, a hundred years before the famine, rich enough to have proper headstones when they died, rich enough to buy fine toys for their children. But a century later they were poor peasants, suffering with a million others all over Ireland when the potato harvests failed.

"How did they fall on such bad times?" said Colin.

Father Hagan shrugged. "I don't know, there's nothing to tell us that. Perhaps someone cheated them out of their land or perhaps—" He paused and looked at Oliver. He may know. He sensed that this boy knew most of the terrible story he was steeling himself to tell them. Oliver rather frightened him.

He went on slowly. "It's hard to believe some of the tales about the famine years, but what happened to the Morrisseys wasn't so unusual."

"What did happen exactly?" Colin asked. "Oliver seems to have read up all about it somewhere, but Prill and I don't understand. What did happen to the old man's family?"

"They starved to death," the priest said flatly. "The last thing they ate would have been their seed potatoes, put by to plant for next year's crop. It was a very simple way of living, you see. They relied on the potato harvest absolutely, to keep going. If that failed them there was nothing. When the seed potatoes had been eaten there would have been nothing left, though some people killed their dogs and ate them, and others ate rats."

"And others fed on the bodies of those that had died," Oliver added. "It was a kind of cannibalism."

"Oliver," Father Hagan said quietly. The boy fell silent. Colin looked across at Prill but her eyes were riveted on the priest's face. Through the window came the hum of voices and the chipping away of spades.

"Just think of it, all the roads to the towns crammed with

starving people, trying to find help. Some fell and died in the ditches, others reached the gates of workhouses and died there. There were so many bodies, not enough coffins for proper funerals. So people remained unburied, or were thrown into great pits.

"And there was disease in the towns, the priests and doctors caught it and died too. Some people survived for quite a long time through begging and stealing. They say the children looked just like monkeys, all wizened and covered with hair. And they lost their powers of speech. In the end they could only open and shut their mouths. No sound came through."

The priest's voice shook, and he stared out of the window. "That field would have been black, as if fire had passed over it. That's how one man described it. And in the hot weather there was an awful smell from the rotting potatoes. The entire harvest had turned black, overnight almost. Imagine it."

But they didn't need to, or the silent, ape-like faces of the children, or the shrivelled women crawling over the potato fields like human scarecrows. They had seen them all. "What about the Morrisseys?" Prill said.

"Well, they were a small family for those days, not many children."

"How many?"

"Four. But by the time they were evicted only three were left, a boy and a girl and a small baby."

"What happened to the fourth?"

"It was the first to die. It had always been weak and it was only a year old. The story goes that the mother took the corpse and left it in the town; she stole a loaf of bread and gave them the dead child instead of money. It was all she had left to give."

He looked into Prill's eyes. He had forgotten that terrible story, unearthed one November afternoon in the university library, so many years ago. Then she had told him about her nightmare, in the stores at Ballimagliesh.

"What does 'evicted' mean?" Colin wanted to know. "What happened to the others?"

"It was when the landlords drove you out of your house," Oliver said, "if you couldn't pay your rent. That's right, isn't it, Father?"

"Yes, Oliver. You're quite right."

He paused again, not knowing how to continue. "It would have been a poor place, of course, not even grand enough to be called a cottage, just a mud cabin shared with pigs and chickens in better days. But it was the only home they had and—" but he stopped again.

"And what, Father Hagan?"

"And it stood here, Colin, here where they built this house."

There was a long silence. Colin and Prill stared at each other, then they both looked at Oliver. When he saw their faces, and knew that they understood, the priest, who had helped people through sickness and death, who had seen all kinds of miseries in Ballimagliesh, felt more helpless than he'd ever done in his life.

Chapter Nineteen

"So that's why everything happened to us," Prill murmured. "It was because we were *here*, in the very spot they'd lived in. We sort of went through it with them, didn't we?"

"And that's why we had to get away," Oliver broke in eagerly. "That's why I had to force you, Prill, because otherwise—"

But Father Hagan was shaking his head. "Let me finish the story now, Oliver." The boy unnerved him. He had an uncanny sense that he understood what had happened far more clearly than anyone else, and that he'd not really needed to look at those old papers, or the university files. But the priest cleared his throat and went on.

"When the Morrisseys were driven out the cabin was destroyed, to stop them coming back. They would have battered the walls in and ripped off the roof, probably set fire to it too."

"And did they kill them?" Prill asked.

"Oh no. Once they'd been got rid of nobody cared what happened to them. The landlords and sheriffs would have moved on then, to root out other poor souls. The Morrisseys obviously went into hiding."

"In that tunnel," Colin broke in. "In that crack below the chapel? That's where they hid, isn't it? I found some initials scratched there, and some bits of writing."

The priest looked very surprised. "Did Donal tell you that? He found his little rattle in that tunnel, and his precious piece of silk. Years ago he discovered those, when he first

177

came here from Kilmacrenan. He knew his family had come from Ballimagliesh and he was determined to find out all about them. And he did. But I'm amazed he told you about those initials in the rock. He's very secretive. It was years before he told me."

"He didn't tell me. It was just a fluke. I was poking about in there with a torch and I climbed up on to a kind of ledge. There were letters scratched into the walls. They said 'Salvation'."

There was another silence and the children waited for the priest to go on. But his soft voice was getting lower and lower. He was slowing down, pushing himself to get to the end, like a man crawling up a rock-face.

"At some point they must have come back, to the ruins of their cabin, and dug themselves a hole to live in, a scalpeen, as Oliver explained. Just a shallow pit, about a metre deep, roofed over with twigs."

"And were they driven out of that as well?"

"No."

"Why not?"

"Because they were dead. They died here, together."

"And nobody buried them?"

"Nobody. The bodies remained in the hole they'd made, in the ruins of the cabin, out there, where Oliver dug his den. In time someone must have come and filled the pit with earth. At least it was a grave."

"But why didn't somebody—" Colin started.

"*Wait*," Oliver said loudly. "He's not finished. There's

something else. Don't interrupt him."

The priest's voice was lighter somehow. "Yes, he's right. Something else, something good, came out of this."

"But *how*?"

"There was a survivor. The baby didn't die. It was found very near death, wailing in the ruins. Someone took it in and cared for it. It was a little girl. She grew up on a farm outside Ballimagliesh. When she married – a cousin, a Michael Morrissey – they went to farm in County Donegal and –"

"And her name was Bridget," Oliver said. "And she was Donal Morrissey's grandmother."

"So it was her voice we heard last night," Prill whispered. "We thought it was Alison. It was their baby, wasn't it, sobbing in the ruins, all those years ago?"

"Did the old man tell you all this?" Colin said, in a choked voice, putting his arm round Prill.

"Yes. He was quite a scholar in his way, and he found out a fair bit about the Morrisseys of Ballimagliesh. After all, Dr Moynihan came here from America to track down his ancestors. Donegal's nearer than New York. Old Donal made his way here years ago, for the same reason."

"So the bones Oliver saw, when it rained, and the child's skull – they think those might be the remains of the Morrissey family?"

"Almost certainly they are. And there's the rattle he dug up, and the scrap of silk. That would help identify them, along with old Donal's relics."

"And what will they do with – with the remains?" Prill

stammered. "When everything's been sorted out?"

"What is usually done," Father Hagan explained calmly. "Graves of this kind have been dug up before. They will bury what they have found in the proper place, and the poor souls will be given their rest."

Outside, the men were leaning on their spades and making signs to the priest. "Well," he said, "I've a feeling they've finished, for now anyway, so I suggest we all—" But a sound cut him off, a shrill, unfamiliar noise that had not been heard for several days. Colin and Prill stood up together, collided in the doorway and fought to get into the hall and along the passage to the kitchen. It was the telephone bell.

Prill got there first. It was a very bad line so she shouted, asking dozens of questions and not hearing a single answer. All she was really listening for was the tone of her mother's voice, to see whether it sounded matter of fact and normal, or horribly emotionless and cold.

"Yes… yes…" she stammered idiotically. Mrs Blakeman sounded quite ordinary. "Something and nothing, love, just a scare in the end," Prill made out, through the crackles. "Hospital tests," she heard. "Marvellous doctor… abnormally high temperature… fluids… quite stable now." Then her father spoke to her, and this time she listened more calmly. "We'll be back tomorrow night," he said. "You'll wait up, won't you? Dr Moynihan's had to go to Amsterdam, anyway, so I'm free for a bit. It'll be pretty late but it will be tomorrow."

Chapter Nineteen

Before they rang off, Father Hagan asked if he could speak too. Prill left him talking. "If you can give me your hotel number I'll ring you back this evening," she heard. "There is something I must tell you. Yes, yes, all quite well now..." he was saying as Prill closed the door and told Oliver the good news about the baby.

Ten minutes later he came off the phone. "I'm sorry your parents won't be back until tomorrow. Perhaps it would be better if you didn't stay here tonight. The O'Malleys are back and they could easily—"

"No. We'll be OK here," Colin said firmly. "We've discussed it between us and we all want to stay. We can get things ready for Mum and Dad. It's settled, isn't it, Prill?"

She nodded. Twenty-four hours ago she'd been determined to leave the place and never come back. But it was different now.

When Father Hagan had gone, the boys went outside to have a look at Oliver's hole. With Jessie plodding slowly after her, Prill wandered round the bungalow, delighting in the ordinariness of everything.

Mrs O'Malley must have been in while they were at Ballimagliesh. There were fresh sheets on the beds and a jug of wild flowers on the kitchen table. All the windows were open and she could smell fields, mixed with soap, furniture polish, and home-made bread. Everything looked welcoming; even the peculiar steel armchairs with their crackly leather covers felt more comfortable. She flopped down in one, and looked through the enormous plate–glass window at the view of cliffs and sea. Now her father was coming she hoped they would stay on. She might even get to like Dr Moynihan's strange pictures in time; they were all blobs and cubes and violent colours, with names like "Dawn" and "Man Sleeping".

"Come on, Jessie," she said, getting up with some difficulty out of the strange chair. "You must practise walking. You'll get fat otherwise." It was most odd having to persuade a dog like Jessie to go for a walk, but she wagged her tail thoughtfully and followed Prill outside, taking a biscuit in her mouth to eat on the way. She only did that when she was pleased.

They went up the farm track together, staggering a little, like two babies learning to walk, or like people recovering from flu. "We must thank Mrs O'Malley for that loaf," Prill told Jessie. "Who knows? We could even cadge something else to eat, if she's been baking. I'm really starting to feel quite hungry."

Chapter Twenty

THE DAY BEFORE the Blakemans went back to England a burial took place in the chapel ruins above Ballimagliesh Strand. When Father Hagan appeared at the gate that led into the overgrown graveyard a small group of people were waiting for him, the O'Malleys, Donal Morrissey, and David Blakeman with the three children. The priest had assured her that it didn't matter, but Mrs Blakeman thought Alison might make a lot of noise and ruin everything, so she was waiting down below, on the beach.

Father Hagan walked through the grass towards them followed by four men carrying a coffin. When they reached the small pool of water that Prill had found, he knelt down, dipped his hand in, and made the sign of the cross. Then he walked on again slowly and stopped at last before an open grave.

Instinctively everybody moved back. The Morrissey headstone had been dug out and laid flat on the ground. Under their feet was a yawning hole and there was a smell of fresh earth and grass. Birds flapped about overhead and a seagull balanced itself on one of the graves, very close to Colin.

It was a highly varnished coffin with brass handles. A plate on the lid said "Morrissey – 1848". It was strange to be so near to it. Last year Colin had gone with his parents to Grandpa Blakeman's funeral but it wasn't like this. Then all he could think about was his funny, tobacco-smelling grandfather being sealed up in that awful container, shut away from them all, for ever. He tried to tell himself that today was different, that this was about a meaningless collection of bones, but when the service started he no longer knew how he felt.

Father Hagan only spoke for a few minutes, first in Latin, then in English. "*Dona eis requiem Domine, et lux perpetua luceat eis*. Give them rest, oh Lord, and let light perpetual shine on them." As she listened, Prill's eyes filled with tears.

When it was over, the men lowered the coffin into the ground on thick ropes. John and Kevin O'Malley bent down and threw handfuls of earth on it, but Donal Morrissey remained upright, swaying slightly as the soil pattered on the polished lid. The farmer's wife tucked her arm through his and walked slowly away with him, along the footpath towards the village.

The Blakemans stood and watched the men shovel earth into the grave. Colin stared down, his hands behind his back.

Chapter Twenty

Oliver peered forward curiously, like a bird. Without thinking, Prill had taken hold of her father's hand. It was too solemn a moment for happiness but inside she was calm. She knew for certain that the peace that had come to the Morrisseys was theirs too.

It was only later, when they sat on the beach eating a picnic, that Prill said what everyone was thinking. Father Hagan didn't look very comfortable somehow, perched on an old bath towel, munching a ham roll, and still wearing his shabby black hat. "Do you think he sleeps in it?" Oliver giggled.

"Why should it have happened when it did?" Prill said. "And why to us?"

The priest was peeling a hard-boiled egg. He took his time over it, then sent Oliver off to get some salt. "Prill, dear, I don't really know. I've thought about it. One possibility is the fact that the new bungalow was only finished a few weeks before you arrived, and you were the first people to live in it. Nobody had lived on that spot since the Morrisseys died, and you were a family, like theirs. You had a small child too. Do you see?"

She shook her head. "But what about the dreams, Father Hagan, and the rottenness of everything? What about those awful nightmares?"

"I know. But sometimes, when there has been violence and great hardship in the past, the power of it reaches out and touches people. What the Morrisseys endured somehow came into your lives, just for those few days. You suffered with them, their pain was your pain. Even when they were dead, and in the pit, you felt the decay, the sense of death."

Prill said nothing. She drew patterns in the sand with one finger, and chewed her lip.

"Just look at Alison," Colin said loudly, thinking that Prill was about to burst into tears. "Look at her hair. She's got yoghurt in it, strawberry yoghurt mixed with sand. Ugh! She's a human disaster area." That made Prill laugh. Then he added, "Perhaps she made it happen."

"Your little sister?" the priest said. "How?"

"Well, don't little kids come into ghost stories sometimes? You know, the kind where things get thrown around? Aren't they supposed to activate things, like chemicals or something?"

"That can't be it," Prill said emphatically. "It got worse when Mum went to Sligo with her, much worse."

Father Hagan wasn't looking at Alison but at Oliver who was running along the beach throwing sticks for Jessie. Colin remembered how he had hated the dog at the beginning of the holiday, and thought how different he was now. He was quite brown. He'd stopped fussing about his clothes and insisting on wearing shoes. He wore some old cut-down jeans of Colin's and a baggy T-shirt advertising Whipsnade Zoo. His small, bare feet made dents in the wet sand. They would miss him when he went back to London.

"I don't know," the priest said. "You could be right. But all kinds of people take babies with them on holiday, and go to places where things have happened in the past. Why should little Alison be special?" His eyes followed Oliver back up the beach. "It could be something quite different. You know, there are people – quite rare, of course –who see more than the rest of us, people who are, well, very sensitive to the feeling of a place. They can often understand its past, and tell you things about it, without ever having been there or anything. They can even tell what's going to happen in the future. That sort of person can stir things up quite innocently, without knowing a thing about it. They don't have to do anything, they're just *there*."

Colin and Prill knew Father Hagan meant Oliver, but neither of them said anything. He spoke briefly to Mum and Dad, shook hands with everybody, and set off up the cliff path. "I'll just look in on old Donal now, thought he looked a bit shaky this morning, didn't you?"

Mrs Blakeman was packing up the picnic. The last three weeks had been sunny and warm, with the odd wet day, but there had been no more of that stifling heat. It was late afternoon now but the sun was still strong. It shone down and made spiky shadows out of the rocks, striping the sand. Then Prill felt cold drops on her face. Rain was starting to fall softly, from a peach-coloured sky.

Oliver came running up with the dog. "Are there any sandwiches left, Auntie Jeannie?" Then he looked up. "Oh heck, it's raining. Oh well, I suppose there would be a rainbow. It's sunny and wet both at the same time, and that's when you get them. So my father says."

And there was, the clearest he had ever seen. They all stood and watched it form, a shimmering arc over the peaceful sea.

Postscript

Books can change your life, and a book that changed mine was *The Great Hunger* by Cecil Woodham Smith. It was published in 1962 and is a factual account of the Irish potato famine of the 1840s. When I read the harrowing descriptions of how the people suffered as they succumbed to starvation conditions and then to death, I wept, and when I had finished the book I remained still for a very long time. Across the years the sufferings of those people had become mine.

The Great Hunger is a masterly account of one of the worst tragedies in human history. For four years the potato crop, which was the staple food of the Irish peasants, was putrefied by blight. The bright green plants became a black harvest as they rotted in the fields, the land stank and the people began to die. In 1845 Ireland was one of the most densely populated countries in Europe; by 1850 it was the thinnest. And it has never recovered.

Most agonising in *The Great Hunger* are the descriptions of children. Starvation turned them into wizened monkey-like creatures covered all over with fine down; hospitals were silent places, filled with iron bedsteads where children opened and shut their mouths noiselessly, waiting for death. Unable to pay the rent, whole families were driven from their pathetic hovels which were then razed to the ground to prevent their return. An eye-witness of such a scene wrote this:

> *At a signal from the sheriff the work began. The miserable inmates of the cabins were dragged out upon the road; the thatched roofs were torn off and the earthen walls battered in by crowbars. The screaming women, the half-naked children, the paralysed grandmother and the tottering grandfather were hauled out. It was a sight I have never forgotten. I was twelve years old at the time, but I think that if a loaded gun had been put into my hand I would have fired into that crowd of villains as they plied their horrible trade. The winter of 1848-49 dwells in my memory as one long night of sorrow.*

When I read *The Great Hunger* I had not published a book, but on the strength of a short ghost story called *Gibsons'* I had been commissioned by HarperCollins to write two "horror" novels. Over the next few years I actually wrote four (*Black Harvest*, *The Beggar's Curse*, *The Witch of Lagg* and *The Pit*). After the fourth I took a long break from creepy stories, but returned to them when I wrote *The Empty Frame*.

I was delighted to be commissioned but was uneasy about horror novels. Horror was a genre I associated with "pulp", with cheap, overblown writing where the author stands on tiptoe throughout to achieve various ghastly effects. I associated it with ectoplasm and mutants, a world in which I had no interest. I decided that any spine-chilling story I might attempt would have to be rooted in reality.

In *The Great Hunger* I found it: a story earthed in human history and more chilling than anything I could invent, so first I created a family in the Enid Blyton tradition. In my own childhood reading I had always looked forward to meeting the same people (and their dogs and cats and parrots) having different adventures. So along came Colin and Prill, their wimpish cousin Oliver, and their dog Jessie. I sent them to Ireland, a country of great beauty which I knew and loved. Mum and Dad came too, and a baby sister, but these I gradually eliminated from the scene so that the three children had centre stage. When young, I was always irked by parents in books who were around too much.

I sent my children not to a sinister cottage with spiders and creaking doors, but to a comfortable seaside bungalow where ghostly happenings were unimaginable. At first they had quiet times, but a series of unexplained and disquieting events began to disturb them until, left alone, they became almost unhinged. In developing my story I drew again and again on *The Great Hunger*. Here I found descriptions of the monkey-like children, of the mother who tried to pay for bread with her dead child, of the skeletal women combing the barren fields for crumbs of food. Here too was the cruel eviction scene described above which supplied the frame for the whole plot. All these things were true.

But I still wanted a happy ending. In the classic ghost story, order is restored only when the troubled dead are in some way comforted. This happens in *Black Harvest* and it is the three children who, having suffered with the famine people, resolve their unquiet and give them their rest. That is why my final image is the biblical one of the rainbow, not a weapon of war but a promise of peace.

Black Harvest was my first published book but, although I have written many since, it is the book with which, to quote Vita Sackville-West, I am "the least dissatisfied". When I wrote it I knew nothing about rules, about "ideal lengths", about "levels of vocabulary". I wrote it in my own way, exactly as it came to me, with an intense, ever-increasing involvement until, in the end, I became my own characters.

The day I finished it I went to visit my next-door neighbour who said, "Goodness, Ann, you're so pale! You look as if you've seen a ghost."

I remember my answer as I sank into a chair. "I've just finished my book about the Irish Famine. Could I possibly have a cup of tea with you?" Because, you see, it was hard to separate myself from the people who had lived with me so long.

Postscript

A storyteller's first aim should surely be to deliver a good read, but I'd like to think *Black Harvest* might also enlarge the sympathies and understanding of those who turn its pages. If it does it will, in its own dark way, have achieved what Robert Frost said a good poem can do, which is to "begin in delight and end in wisdom".

ANN PILLING